~Valley Fever

# Valley Fever

~

## (Where Murder Is Contagious)

A COLLECTION OF SHORT STORIES SET IN
THE SAN JOAQUIN VALLEY

Sunny Frazier

JoAnne Lucas

Cora Ramos

2003 · Fithian Press, McKinleyville, California

Published by Fithian Press
A division of Daniel and Daniel, Publishers, Inc.
Post Office Box 2790
McKinleyville, CA 95519
www.danielpublishing.com

LIBRARY OF CONGRESS CATALOGING-IN-PUBLICATION DATA
Lucas, JoAnne.
  Valley fever : mystery stories set in central California / by JoAnne Lucas,
Sunny Frazier, and Cora Ramos.
     p. cm.
  ISBN 1-56474-428-0 (pbk. : alk. paper)
  1. Detective and mystery stories, American—California—Central Valley
(Valley) 2. Central Valley (Calif. : Valley)—Fiction. I. Frazier, Sunny.
II. Ramos, Cora. III. Title.
  PS648.D4L83 2003
  813'.08720807945—dc21
       2003010146

*To the inspiration and memory of Karen Besecker,
and the guidance of Elnora King*

# Contents

~Valley Fever

# Murderous Martini

JO ANNE LUCAS

Clear and potent in a crystal glass chilled,
A lacing of poison for the next to be killed.
A touch of vermouth, more generous with gin—
A toast and a promise, let the murders begin.

~

# ~FINE DI*E*XING~

# A Tale of Two Sittings

SUNNY FRAZIER

It was the best of crimes, it was the worst of crimes.

It was a crime so well thought out, so magnificent in execution, I had to admire the murderers. Passion prompted the act, vanity was its undoing.

I was twenty-one at the time, an English major at the local university, with a very minor in costume design. To earn tuition, I was forced to wait on tables. I consoled myself that my servitude took place in the toniest eatery in Fresno, California. The Daily Planet dished up California cuisine along with a retro atmosphere. The thirties were alive and kickin' within the art deco bistro. The tips weren't bad either.

One of the perks of the job was waiting tables for the monthly get-together of a group of mystery writers known as the Deadly Dames. They met like clockwork the first Saturday of the month. It was my job to keep the iced tea and coffee flowing, and the Sweet'N Low stocked in the sugar bowls.

But these weren't the usual ladies-who-lunch. They plotted murder as they noshed. From the grandma pondering arsenic poisoning to the young gospel singer intent on offing a blackmailer, these women were out to kill. They forked up watercress as the coroner flashed slides of homicides across the screen; they nibbled focaccia during a forensic lecture on rigor mortis. Nothing fazed this group.

But for every perk, there is an equal and opposite non-perk. That's how I felt when management presented me with my new uniform: tuxedo pants and double-breasted bolero jacket, topped off with a pillbox hat. I looked like an usherette, which was the idea. Next door to the restaurant was a renovated movie house and my boss was trying his best to attract the theater crowd. The outfit was an embarrassment, but one I only had to suffer on the nights I worked the back room.

That's where I was working on the fateful Friday. The late-night crowd filled the section to capacity. There were five waitresses working, but I had the back room to myself. Which meant I had to keep an eye on the privacy booths. The curtained dining areas were atmospheric, but a nightmare for a waitress. Customers flicked on a discreet blue light for service, which was hard to spot on a busy night. And I was required to punch a warning buzzer before pushing the curtain aside and bringing in the food. I tried hard not to think about the shenanigans going on when the curtains were drawn.

By the end of the night in question, my pillbox was askew and the strap cut into my neck. I only had one more table to clear—the privacy booth in the back. That's when I saw the blue light. Odd. I remembered the couple leaving ten minutes earlier. They were a distinctive pair, dressed to match the surroundings: he, in a wide-lapel suit and fedora; she, in a straight skirt and peplum jacket. I'd seen the outfit at Macy's just the week before. But the hat she wore was vintage—gray felt with a thick veil that made her look smoky and mysterious. Her blond French twist peeked out from underneath it.

I pressed the buzzer, waited, then pushed aside the curtain. The woman lay across the banquette, her eyes in a dead stare, one hand reaching for the light switch.

She definitely wasn't ordering seconds on dessert.

My scream brought everybody running. Someone called 911.

While I waited for the police to arrive, I played back the evening in my head. The woman and her boyfriend had ordered scampi, drunk Chablis, fed each other rolls. She lifted her veil, but didn't remove the hat. It seemed to me like an awkward way to dine. I remembered her blood-red fingernails brushing crumbs seductively from her crimson mouth. That's all I saw because they kept the curtain closed through the rest of the meal.

But I caught a glimpse of the woman as she was walking back from the ladies' room. I remembered she reached up to adjust the veil.

Her fingernail polish was gone.

When I told this story to the homicide detectives, they shrugged it off.

"The lady still has red nails," Detective Reynoso pointed out.

It was true. Her fingers were turning blue, making the red stand out even more.

"Maybe she gave herself a manicure between the main course and dessert," the detective suggested.

Only a man would come up with that theory, but I let it slide. Instead, I searched under the table and around the booth for the gray felt hat.

"I saw her leave the restaurant, and she was wearing the hat." I looked at Reynoso, but his face was an unreadable mask. He had my statement and was done with me.

As the police busied themselves with the crime scene, I thought through the evening. The disappearing manicure, the phantom hat, a woman who returned to the restaurant sans husband. None of it made sense.

Then it hit me.

Somewhere between the stuffed mushroom appetizers and the Chocolate Sin Cheesecake, there'd been a switcheroo. I went back to the detective and explained to Reynoso that another woman, dressed in the same exact outfit, must have slipped in the back door next to the bathroom. She'd left with the man on her arm, the hat on her head, and a corpse in her wake.

"If you find the hat, you'll find the impostor," I told Reynoso. "She helped the man pull off the murder."

"And just how are we supposed to find one hat in a city of four hundred thousand people?" he snorted.

"Maybe you should put out an All Points Bulletin," I suggested. "No woman in her right mind would destroy such a great hat."

Reynoso wasn't buying the Sidney Carton scenario. "You've been reading too many murder mysteries," he said as he followed the body bag to the coroner's wagon.

The unsolved murder made headlines and business died. Nobody wanted to eat at a restaurant with death on the menu. The Daily Planet became known as The Daily Panic. The only clients who didn't desert us were the Deadly Dames. They savored the notoriety along with the radicchio salad.

I saw her six months later at one of their meetings. The theme of the luncheon was "Hanging Out with Dashiell Hammett," and everyone was dressed in period attire. They were talking *Thin Man* and eating heavy. She had the same French twist, only this time she was a brunette. The hat was a dead giveaway.

I ran to the phone and dialed 911. The homicide detectives arrived. One cuffed her while another recited the *Miranda*. The Deadly Dames didn't know whether to applaud or be appalled. Some scribbled notes for future storylines.

The headline in the paper called it a crime of passion. She confessed her lover slipped Rohypnol (known on the street as "Roofies") into his wife's wine. The dose was large enough for the date-rape drug to cause paralysis and, ultimately, death.

Later that day, I went to police headquarters and pestered Detective Reynoso for any details the newspaper left out.

"You were right on target with your theory," he told me. There was no mistaking the grudge in his tone.

"How did they pull it off?"

"When the drug got into his wife's system, he took off her hat and slipped it under his jacket. Then he went over to the back door and let his mistress in. She stated she made a pit stop in the ladies' room to adjust the hat and veil," Reynoso told me.

"What about the fingernail polish?"

"She forgot about the manicure until it was too late. She didn't figure anybody would pay much attention."

Except me. I could imagine the rest of the scene. The faux wife slipped into the privacy booth, ate cheesecake, and waited for the real wife to die. She was clearly a fashion accessory to murder.

According to Reynoso, forensics determined that after the murderer and his mistress left the scene, the real Mrs. managed to regain consciousness long enough to press the light for service. It was too late—the only service she got was a funeral.

It didn't take long for the accomplice to rat out her boyfriend. He was arrested in San Francisco, running a vintage clothing store.

But there's a happy ending to the tale. I was made an honorary Deadly Dame. As a result, I gave up the classics, studied the mystery genre, and penned a series about a yodeling private eye in the Canadian Rockies. It won the Shamus and I quit my night job.

Writing murder mysteries is, to misquote Dickens, a far, far better thing I do than waiting tables.

~

# A Feast for Fools

JO ANNE LUCAS

The lights went out and down I went, pushed in the face by some lime-scented clown. I felt my skirt catch on something and rip. In our restaurant there were the usual crashes and cries you get with sudden darkness, but after I made body contact with the carpet, I also heard the tinkling of bells.

An eerie glow caught my eye and disappeared; I groped for the wall, fingered my way to the main light switch, and pushed the toggle up.

The scenario was bad for business.

Throughout our dining room, customers in their costumes resembled revelers at some mad Mardi Gras. One of them might be the unknown newspaper columnist I feared; the one who delighted in reporting any little factor that might contribute to a poor dining performance. And our big headline-maker right now featured Trevor Sorenson, sprawled backwards in his chair on the floor. A knife skewered the large boutonniere on his breast.

Boy, this is a tough way to make a buck. I'd told Jeff earlier there'd be trouble....

"It's a blasted setup, that's what it is. I can smell it." My brother didn't respond, so I slapped a wooden spoon down hard against the kitchen counter top, then waved it under his nose.

"Look, who else would make such a screwy reservation? First he picks our busiest night in six weeks, next he demands that particular table in the alcove, then the main course must be finished before a quarter to twelve, and you have to come out of the kitchen precisely then to receive your accolades. Accolades! That's the word the turkey buzzard used. This *has* to be a sneak review by that blasted Eccentric Gourmet!" I whacked the spoon again, and it broke.

"Dorothy, Dorothy, don't get so worked up." Jeff took the ruined utensil from me and shook his head. "Here, try the pâté, it's Lucullan."

I stuffed my mouth with chopped liver on toast and watched him perform magic with his knife. In two minutes flat he'd abracadabra'd one basket of whole limes into neat slices for the salmon's court bouillon and carved another basket of limes into the entre's side garnishes.

I swallowed my last bite. "All I'm saying is that everything must be perfect. No, better than perfect. Everything must be marvelously magnificent tonight."

"I am always magnificent. Tonight will only be more of the same." He pointed his knife at me. "You fuss too much."

I sniffed; I'm not the one who swoons over a bruised banana. The gods of the gene pool must have been feeling frisky when they wafted their wands over us. Hercules-huge and gentle as mother's love, Jeff is profoundly passionate about foods, fine wines, and country music. I am younger, smaller, and prettier, with an appetite for bookkeeping, business, and bank accounts.

I argued some more, but I couldn't get beneath Jeff's culinary concerns. He checked ovens, washed greens, and worried pots on the gas range. He slowed his choreography long enough to say, "The Eccentric Gourmet will not be dining here tonight, so no bad review. We *will* be late seating our first diners, and that will be your fault. Move it, girl. Go charm the customers and leave the kitchen to me. I promise I will be magnificent...as always."

I slammed the swinging door behind me so it flapped a few times and put on my best hostess smile. Arrogance is all very well for a chef, but it doesn't guarantee the bank balance.

The swanky San Joaquin Country Club up the road always holds an All Fools' Ball the Saturday night nearest April first, and tonight was March 31st. Discerning members dine here, then join the festivities. All dress as clowns and crown a King of Fools at two A.M.

In keeping with the event I wore the feminine version of a Pierrot costume, a sexy powder-puff number with legs. My irritation with the neck ruff competed with my worry about the mysterious restaurant reviewer. A fierce storm outside made me shiver behind my reception desk and curse eighteenth-century clowns for not being brighter about Thermals. The only good thing about my position here tonight was that it backed into the bay alcove.

I worked my troubleshooting bit on all manner of clowns—Bozos, Harlequins, amorous buffoons—your typical Saturday night crowd. My suspect reservation for four arrived at ten-thirty. I led them to their table while I studied each; an Emmett Kelly hobo, a pudgy Pagliacci, Batman's Joker, and Rigoletto, the hump-backed court jester in motley dress and bells. Pagliacci introduced the nattily dressed Joker as Trevor Sorenson, our famous local syndicated talk-show host who raked his guests live over their burning goals and served them up as toast. The hobo clown wrote for the show, surly Rigoletto directed it, and hefty Pagliacci produced it.

Theirs was the last reservation for the night, and I personally waited their table. I eyed Trevor Sorenson again; with his white makeup and green wig he positively oozed evil glee.

I poured wine for all with a lavish hand and sent up "Please, please" prayers for everything to go right. A verbal basting of us on Sorenson's show would be worse than any old nosy newspaper report. His aired opinions often contained poisoned slashes, seldom grounded in fact. Jeff's friend and former employer, Auguste Georges, had to close down after just such a blast. I decided I would pray and I would please, but I would not grovel.

Which posed the question of how to deal with him on a personal level. He was Hollywood-handsy. Usually I left some slapped male anatomy behind me as a hint of my displeasure. This time I opted for sweet talk and fast footwork and between courses I kept my ears on them from my desk.

Sorenson proved a horrible host. He taunted Rigoletto about keeping his hands wrapped around a bottle and letting wife number four slip through his fingers. The jester responded by knocking back a full glass of wine. And though lashed for being a wimp, a hanger-on, and a loser, the little hobo clown remained speechless.

I tried to lighten the uneasy ambience by making a big production with the main course. I served Pagliacci poached salmon and tempted the Emmett Kelly with our apple-and-sage stuffed capon. I placed wild boar stew in front of Rigoletto and presented a superb *boeuf* Wellington to Joker Sorenson. Each dish was a masterpiece of taste, aroma and appearance, and I anticipated their compliments.

But Rigoletto brushed his dish to the side and gestured for more wine. From my desk I watched the Emmett Kelly merely push his food around the plate. Pagliacci wolfed his dinner, played with the garnishes, and eyed Rigo's neglected stew. However, Sorenson ate with appetite and enthusiasm and filleted Pagliacci about his reversal of fortune. Pagliacci's face and white clown costume matched; he burped his indignation.

When Ramón cleared the dishes, the clock showed twenty minutes to midnight.

"What's for dessert, doll?" Sorenson asked.

"Gooseberry Fool, of course," I said.

"Perfect. Before you bring it out, babe, I want the bottle of champagne opened, and bring six glasses. I'm going to make an important announcement, and I want you to stick around. Oh, and, honey, tell the cook he can come, too." He gave my leg a squeeze and my tush a slap to send me on my way.

I was hot enough to boil water, but icy breaths of worry cooled me when I wondered about the champagne's purpose: toast or roast?

I hadn't mentioned to Jeff yet that Sorenson was here. Big Brother had really carried on when Auguste was forced to move. Jeff's reactions now to Sorenson's summons made me long to share a Maalox Moment with Pagliacci; Jeff looked dangerous.

On my return trip through the dining room I noted the few diners left were well into the coffee-and-dessert stage. Good, I thought, as soon as I get rid of my clowns, I'll ace these frou-frou pumps and reintroduce my feet to comfort.

The men had left the table and stretched. They still stood about, with Sorenson posturing by his chair. I poured the champagne and handed him the first glass.

"Thanks, doll face, pour one for yourself.... Gentlemen and lovely lady," he began. He nattered on about how he was born on the first day of April and how April had always been his lucky month. Rigoletto muttered something about it not being April yet. Sorenson ignored him. He went on to say that April first used to be New Year's Day and that he'd always made his important moves on that day.

"...and since this is the end of the last day of March, and— ah, I see the cook is joining us. Pour another glass, sweet lips, and let us all drink—"

I reached for the champagne bottle, and that's when the lights went out.

A sheriff's detective dressed as a burlesque clown was among the late diners. This proved to be our one big break of the day. He secured the crime scene, separated suspects and witnesses, and removed his red rubber nose. Because he'd been present and knew the setup, he got right down to the nitty-gritty: Where were you when the lights went out?

I'd been the closest to Sorenson, but the coroner stated I couldn't have shoved the knife that hard into the corpse's chest. Off the cuff, Dr. Wallis speculated that to have penetrated that deeply, most likely the knife was thrown. But how it hit its mark in the dark was the detective's job to find out.

Fear for Jeff tangled with my thoughts, and I had to really concentrate while Pagliacci and Rigoletto told their stories. I closed my eyes to free my senses. Pagliacci burped.

Bingo! My eyes flashed my triumph and connected with the detective's. "All right, Miss Felcher," he said, "let's hear from you."

I moved over by him. "Let's say Sorenson stood where you are, and I'm here, at right angles on your left. Now the lights go out, and at the same time, Mr. Producer here pushes me down."

Pagliacci protested, but I tell how he's the only one in the vicinity at that time who's had fresh limes to squeeze for the fish entrée, and I had smelled the limes on his hands.

He sputtered that whoever cut and handled the limes would smell, too. No way, I told him; Jeff also dealt with garlic, onions, and herbs, and I only smelled the limes.

The detective sniffed Jeff's hands, then Pagliacci's. He stated for the record his findings to be as I'd said. "But, what's the big deal about pushing you down?" he asked.

"Not so much down," I answered slowly, "more like out of the way. Tinkle Toes over there is the wise guy who threw the light switch. I heard his bells behind me."

"The dame's screwy," Rigoletto said.

The detective paced and recapped. "So, you say the jester turns off the lights, and this guy pushes you out of the way, then that leaves—"

We all turned to the Emmett Kelly clown. The little hobo nodded and stared at his hands. Tears smeared his makeup.

"But," argued the detective, "how could he do it? He'd have to have thrown blind, no light, no target—"

"He had a target," I said, "that big fake flower on Sorenson's lapel, it glowed in the dark. I remember thinking it must be some kind of gnarly fungus to match his personality."

Pagliacci finally admitted to everything. Trevor Sorenson's present contract expired today; he was leaving the show and moving to network TV and New York. The producer arranged for the costumes and added the glow-in-the-dark boutonniere. The three men had intended to murder him at the ball where there would be more people around, but Sorenson took too long over dinner and with his toast. Sorenson's planned move was a monetary disaster for Pagliacci; however, the producer held a key-man insurance policy on the TV star that lapsed at midnight on March 31st.

Rigoletto hated Sorenson for seducing his wife and laughing about it. Rigo wasn't about to let Sorenson move away from him and his revenge.

"And, what about you?" the detective asked the little hobo.

Kelly straightened his shoulders and spoke for the first time. "I loved him."

Whew! I thought, better him than me.

Much later, I sipped cappuccino in the office. Jeff alternated between staring at the wall and writing furiously. I asked what he was doing.

"Tonight's events make a review by the Eccentric Gourmet necessary to bring the restaurant's reputation back into balance. Sorenson was killed for his deeds, not my food."

I spilled my coffee. "You? You? But, why?"

He gave that little shrug that makes me want to shake him. "I decided to make dining out seem more adventurous. People became excited by the mystery. It was good for business, right?" Jeff was exactly right, and always being right is what had frightened me about the Eccentric Gourmet.

The wind died, and I listened to rain stamp its tiny feet.

Well, well. So Jeff couldn't keep his fingers out of my end of the pie. Typical older brother stunt, got a big laugh out of my freaking out earlier.

I poured more coffee and sauntered across the room to read over his shoulder.

"The column needs punching up," I said, "add some spice to it. Start out with, 'It was a dark and stormy night,' and put in about the costumes. Oh, and mark your calendar for Tuesday. I want to case Romero's Ristorante for next week's piece. We'll get some good material there."

Jeff threw down his pen and looked affronted, offended, and pushed. Too bad. Brothers everywhere need to be taught that little sisters add the à l'orange to life's ducks.

I opened the drapes to a watery dawn. The Day of Fools was going to be a beautiful day.

~

# Out of the Frying Pan

SUNNY FRAZIER

The television newscaster cracked open an egg and deposited the contents on the pavement. "One hundred and twelve degrees," announced the reporter. Jeannie Siddons, hand on hip, mouthed his next words: "Hot enough to fry an egg on the sidewalk."

"A waste of a good egg," muttered her boss. Mr. Vartikian wasted nothing in the hole-in-the-wall diner he owned on C Street—with the exception of his entire life.

Jeannie had other plans. She thought of those plans as she wiped the lunch counter, expending as little energy as possible. All she needed was enough money to fix the radiator on the '82 Pontiac, and she'd leave Fresno for good. Next time she'd steal a car in better condition. Next time she'd break down in a cooler part of California.

Meanwhile, she was stuck in the only job she could find on short notice. Mr. Vartikian's idea of a job interview was to check out her legs and bustline, not bothering to ask if she had previous experience as a waitress. Which she didn't, but what could people expect from a nineteen-year-old? Anyway, the old man was getting what he paid for, which was next to nothing.

The polyester uniform Mr. Vartikian insisted she wear clung to her body like a damp rag, and it was only noon. If only the man would turn on the damn air conditioner instead of trying to save a dime by running the ceiling fans! Jeannie took the dish towel and mopped perspiration off her face.

"Psst! Jeannie. You think it's hot out there, come back to the kitchen." Tino's brown face peered through the service window as he pushed two plates through. Grilled cheese. BLT. Fries looking limp and dripping with oil. She gagged as she handed the food to two men who looked like their last meal came from the garbage bin out back. No tip here.

The C Street Diner attracted the poor and nutritionally challenged. Jeannie knew about scrounging for food, having grown up one of seven children to a single mom who was drunk more often then employed. Still, there were limits. She couldn't stomach most of the food served by Vartikian, even when she wasn't fighting morning sickness twenty-four hours a day.

She went around to the kitchen where Tino stood in a cloud of steam, hot dishwater reaching halfway up his arms.

"I saved you a roast beef sandwich. The bread's fresh." He nodded to a plate covered with a napkin. "Eat it quick while old man Vartikian isn't looking. I'll tell him you stepped out back for a smoke break."

"Thanks, Tino." She gave him a kiss on the back of the neck where the rubber band circled his ponytail.

"Come dancing with me tonight. The Red Parrot has maria-chis and nice, cool margaritas."

"It's too hot to dance," she replied. The service phone in the kitchen rang and Tino did a few fancy dance steps over to it. Jeannie snatched up the sandwich on her way out the back door. Sitting on the stoop next to the Dumpster, Jeannie ate the sand-wich and plotted her next move. Leaving Gerald before the next beating had been her only goal when she swiped his car and headed up Highway 99, leaving Bakersfield and her hus-band of two weeks in the dust. She wanted to get out of the Valley and go north, someplace green. Maybe Shasta. That sounded cool, like the soda pop.

Bakersfield was hotter than hell, but nothing like Fresno. It felt as if the devil had turned up the burner under the city. The TV was full of gang shootings and grass fires—that is, when the news people weren't frying eggs to prove it was hot. She took the last bite of her sandwich and licked mayonnaise off her fingers.

The Pontiac made her even hotter than the pavement. Gerald probably had reported it stolen by now; she'd have to lift a set of plates before she headed out of town. Meanwhile, she kept the junker parked behind the restaurant during the day and in an alley behind the motel at night.

The door to the old walk-in freezer was propped open with a wooden crate. Jeannie accidently kicked it as she hurried by.

"Hey!" Tino poked his head out of the freezer. "If you knock the box away, I'll be trapped in here until I'm a Popsicle!" The hinges were worn and the heavy door no longer stayed open on its own. The safety lock on the inside was also broken.

"Then I'll lick you until you disappear."

Mr. Vartikian picked that moment to walk up behind her. "Don't talk trash to the kitchen help," he snapped. "Get those tables cleared before the afternoon rush. I'm not paying you to waste time."

Afternoon rush? Jeannie bore down on the tables with a vengeance. The old buzzard must think more than two people in the place was a "rush." And with the wages he was paying, she could waste the whole day and still come up short in her paycheck.

When she returned to the kitchen, Tino grabbed her dishrag. "Don't let him get to you. You gotta keep your cool or you'll blow like a volcano."

"If I didn't need the money so bad, I'd leave this dump right in the middle of rush hour—whenever that's supposed to be!"

He laughed and pulled her close. "I like a woman with fire. Come dancing with me tonight."

"Tino!" Vartikian stood in the doorway, his arms loaded with dirty dishes. He slammed them down on the counter. "I've warned you once. Collect your pay and get the hell out!"

Tino whipped off his apron and threw it on the floor. He winked at Jeannie as he walked out the back door. But Vartikian wasn't through.

"You want to fool around on my time, you can stay late and clean up the kitchen every night until I find a replacement for Tino. I'll get someone who can keep his hands to himself."

Without Tino's jokes and flirting, the day dragged by. No one showed up at the dinner hour. Jeannie nursed three Coca-Colas to fight the nausea from eating the sandwich. Vartikian deducted the price of the sodas from her pay.

Finally finished scrubbing the dishes, she took off her apron and hung it on a nail in the wall. She smelled of old grease and sweat, and looked forward to the relief of a cold shower. All she needed was her pay. She looked for the old man. The door of the freezer was propped open with the crate.

"I suppose you want your money," said Vartikian. He stood deep in the recesses of the freezer, next to cheap cuts of meat stacked on a shelf. Reaching into his pocket, he pulled out a twenty and a ten-dollar bill. He held it out to her. "Come in and get it."

She stepped a little way into the freezer. "That's not enough money. I did Tino's work, too."

"I wouldn't complain, if I were you. I had my poker buddy, Leo, check out that Pontiac you drive. He's a retired cop. Turns out the car is stolen. One phone call and I could put you behind bars." He reached out to grab her. "Convince me not to make that call."

Maybe it was an accident; maybe it was in the back of her mind all along. In her rush to get away, she kicked the crate loose from its place. The freezer door swung shut. Mr. Vartikian pressed his face against the small window. He was yelling something, probably obscenities.

Jeannie's hand hovered over the door handle. Thirty dollars for a day's work and overtime! She deserved better. Opportunity was as close as the cash register.

The only light in the restaurant was early evening sun filtering through the drawn blinds. The register responded to her touch, opening with a clatter of coins. For a slow day, there was still enough in the till to get her out of town. Underneath the change drawer was an extra stash of two hundred dollars. Maybe she'd dump the car and catch the first bus leaving Fresno.

Jeannie heard a noise behind her and whirled around.

"What's going on, girl?" Tino stood in the doorway.

"What are you doing here?"

"I came to take you dancing." He held out his hand.

Her damp palms clutched the money. "I can't go with you. I have to catch a bus."

"I saw what you did to Vartikian."

She said nothing. Stuffing the money in the pockets of her polyester dress, Jeannie started past Tino. He grabbed her arm.

"We can go dancing anywhere you want. I got a car, no job, nothing to keep me here. I'm as free as you are."

Free. For the first time she felt it, a sense of freedom. A few laws had to be broken to get there, but it was worth the risk. All she had to do now was get as far away from Fresno as possible.

"Take me to someplace cold," she said.

"Baby, I'll take you to the North Pole. We'll dance on the ice!"

Arms around each other, they walked through the kitchen. Vartikian pounded on the thick glass. Jeannie ignored him. She needed a head start to put some distance between herself and the police. She knew the old man would be fine. Leo was due to arrive in twenty minutes to pick him up for the weekly card game.

She walked out without noticing the scribbled message canceling the poker party. It was sitting on the counter right where Tino left it.

~

32

# Motive, Means, and Ooops!

JO ANNE LUCAS

Poison is always risky; even Quinidine, that lovely heart medicine left over from my dear late husband. Oh well, no pain—no gain.

The elegant new dining room at the Daily Planet Restaurant was filled with the noisy banter of thirty-eight mystery writers. Pleasant table attendants replenished tall goblets with iced tea and pottery mugs with fragrant hot coffee. We were meeting that afternoon for a lunch and lecture with Eileen Holmes, who would speak on "Sewing Patterns for Your Stories."

Amelia Satterbourn buttonholed me along with our president, Carrie Beacons, and others so she could gas away about her latest opus sent to Ballantine. Her work is showing an irritating tendency to garner acceptance from publishers. Her vocalized preening on the subject always screeches up the scales to the heights of stridency. I'm afraid I find her shrillness is only equaled in unpleasantness by her constant smug reminders that she alone is *the* published author of consequence in our group.

Amelia let go of my arm, set her iced tea on the table, and swooped over to corner the newspaper columnist who covers our meetings and so to relate, ad infinitum, all she had told before. Would we ever get to hear dear Eileen tell us how to guilt a quilt?

Our Carrie donned her presidential mantle and made Amelia sit down in her assigned place. Amelia grumbled and reached for her goblet. In anticipatory exuberance, Bunny Branz kicked my ankle under the table. Imagine my surprise when sweet Eileen, seated next to Amelia, suddenly choked. Her face turned a rosy hue before she slumped to the floor. Dear me, had I made a tiny miscalculation? I glanced around the room where thirty-five pairs of eyes glared at me. Totally oblivious, Amelia stood up and started opening remarks to the effect that she would take over today's presentation—again.

Three dozen sorely tried writers telegraphed a desperate S.O.S. As I settled myself in my chair, I knocked a cup of coffee onto Amelia's skirt. Tsk-tsk, such a clumsy wuss! I brushed Amelia down with a napkin and led her out of the dining area to the ladies' restroom. I'm afraid I gushed a bit to detract her attention while I gave the group a thumbs-up behind my back.

"Amelia dear, have we ever discussed how many of today's fatal accidents actually occur in the bathroom?"

~

# ~VALLEY HEAT~

# Too Hot To Handle

CORA J. RAMOS

Detective Mac Mullain swore at the temperature gauge as he came down off the Grapevine onto the San Joaquin Valley floor. The temperature outside read one hundred fifteen, his car was overheating, and it felt like Death Valley inside.

"Just my luck the air conditioner had to give me trouble today."

He hoped the car would cool coming down off the foothills, but somewhere between Wheeler Ridge and Mettler, the engine began knocking. He took the next off-ramp and drove until he saw an old tin-roofed bar with a flickering neon sign that said, "OLD BEER."

"I hope that means cold." He needed to cool down as much as the car. He'd already been sweating at the thought of apologizing to Darla. Now the fates were conspiring against him to put the heat on big-time. The dark thought amused him as he stood inside the doorway a moment to let his eyes adjust to the dimness. He breathed in the air conditioning as he moved to the bar and ordered a beer.

Maybe Darla was right—he should transfer out of Vice. Time to come back into the real world of honest dealings and normal living. He'd gotten so used to the dark, seedy world that truthfulness had fallen by the wayside.

The bartender set the bottle down and Mac swallowed a

third of it in one long gulp. Then he heard the voices in the booth in back of him.

"The hell you say! I'm no snitch. Ain't no way I'm gonna tell Sadie about ol' Sal stepping out on her. She finds out, I don't plan on being nowhere closer'n shoutin' distance. She's thrown more than one pot at me."

Mac checked out the reflections of the two men in the mirror over the bar.

"You crazy, Petey, for even suggesting it." The short, fat man slammed the long-neck down on the table and sat back against the torn vinyl booth.

"Okay, Corky, say you're right," goaded the thin, gaunt man across from him. "Then how we gonna get the dough to get up north to do the deed? Huh? We need ten bucks for gas and Sadie's the only one around here to get it from. She sure ain't gonna *loan* it to us. If we don't get there soon, we're out five big ones. When's the last time you saw that much money?"

"How you figure Sadie's gonna give me ten bucks?"

"'Cause when you tell her about Sal, she'll dish it out to know where he's at."

"Nooo—no way, man. Sal'll kill me sure."

Mac couldn't make out Petey's deep-set eyes, but sensed they were cold and lifeless. The two deadbeats continued. He tried not to listen. Didn't want to get involved. He was off duty and heading home to Darla. It had been six days since he'd last seen her. Last time he talked to her, she was fuming mad.

"So why's this broad want someone to dim her old man's lights anyway?" Corky belched. "He been stepping out on her?"

"Naw, man, when Gino set it up, she told him she was tired of her old man's shit or something. Probably wants insurance. Classy dames don't kill for hurt feelings. When they get mad they go for the money, man." Petey spread his arms wide. "Big insurance policies."

38

"And we gonna *go for* it, too," Corky's high-pitched giggle echoed through the bar.

Mac was so tired of having to deal with these types—always shucking and jiving, always trying some new angle to make a buck, always illegal. If he heard much more he'd feel obligated to get involved, but it was too hot to handle these creeps. What could he do anyway? Arrest them for talking? They'd probably just keep arguing and procrastinating until they ended up drunk and useless. This wasn't his jurisdiction anyway.

Empty promises—it's what he'd given Darla for too many years—never quite doing what he said, always half-assed and minimal. This trip had been a turning point and soon he'd be home and he could show her he meant business this time.

Corky got up and went through the door marked "Phones." Mac stopped trying to figure out their next move and ordered a whiskey with a beer chaser.

It'd been ten days since Darla had given him the ultimatum—divorce, if he didn't get out of Vice. He'd appeased her, handed her a cubic zirconia ring and a life insurance policy that assured her she'd be well taken care of if anything happened to him. After she'd given him that funny look, he felt bad. She deserved more than a marriage that was a sidebar to his career.

"Okay, man, it's on." Corky had come back. "We gotta go. Sadie's gonna give me the ten." They continued in hushed tones, then got up and left.

Mac went to the phone and called home. When Darla didn't answer he called her sister. Sometimes she spent the night there when she was upset with him. Darla answered.

"Honey, I'm sorry for all I've put you through." She was silent. He continued, "Listen, I know I've lied and disappointed you—put our marriage on hold for too long—but I had this revelation and I'm going to make things right." He told her he now realized how wrong he'd been.

She listened quietly. "If you're *really* serious this time, come

39

and pick me up, now, before you do anything else. Don't go home—come straight here."

"Sure, honey, whatever you want. Things will be different. I'll be back on the road as soon as the car cools. Figure about two and a half, three hours before I can get there."

He hung up knowing he'd fudged a little, but it was only because he had to stop at the house first, pick up his credit card for a real nice gift to take to her.

By the time Mac pulled into his driveway, he'd been anticipating the evening ahead—Darla's smile, her kisses, her soft, warm body against him. He unlocked the door and saw the light in the back. Darla knew him too well. She'd come home to surprise him. He hurried down the hall anticipating her, when the two dark figures stepped into the hallway.

He heard the high-pitched laugh and made the connection too late. Three quick flashes and the thin man stepped out of the shadows as Mac sank to the floor.

Everything went into slow motion for Mac as Petey came toward him holding a gun. He'd been wrong about Darla... hadn't taken her threats seriously. He'd been wrong about the men and their determination. He'd even been wrong about himself—his ability to change. He'd been right about one thing, though, Petey's cold, lifeless eyes....

~

# Killer Tan

JO ANNE LUCAS

"Die, you weasly chartreuse varmit!"

I hit it with a stream from the sprayer. The ugly little rascal sat up on its many hindquarters and gestured for me to "Put 'em up."

I shot it again, but Superworm still inched toward the rich promise of a ripening tomato. I headed it off at the pass and we grappled in hand-to-hand combat. A car came up the driveway. The driver tooted his horn and my tomato worm dropped down into a jungle of plant leaves on the ground. I vowed to return.

I was staying in the apartment over the garage while Stella, my late father's second wife, jetted around to better climes. I watched over the house and took care of the vegetable garden and Dad's roses during the hot months of a Fresno summer. Stella's too cheap to hire a full-time gardener to see to the grounds, only a lawn service for surface appearances. Dad always took pride in his rose garden, so I've kept it up since his sudden death two years ago. Fall time, I returned to my dorm at Fresno State University.

Dad's will stipulated Stella to be the sole executrix and my guardian until I marry (only with her consent) or reach the age of twenty-five. So Stella carried my love life, allowance, and inheritance in her graspy little hands. Since I'm only twenty now, she would continue to pay herself an increasingly outrageous salary as executrix and live in my father's house for another five years. Forget my getting married, she's already nixed or lured away every prospective boyfriend I've brought around. Poor Dad, he must have had some really gnarly middle-aged crisis thing after Mom died. What else explained his marrying a she-devil of a woman only six years older than I? I guess I would get along with her better if she'd made Dad happy. But it didn't happen. Plus, she can make me feel like a bad-hair-day every time I'm around her.

My visitor, Hugh Dearing, the family lawyer, waited for me on my little porch. I quickly washed up and moved a small wicker table and chairs around outside to catch the breeze. Besides having the personality of wet newspaper, Hugh wrote up Dad's last will and was a frequent guest of Stella's. He cleared his throat to signal the beginning of some lawyerly pronouncement.

"Er, you know Stella went on a trip to Mexico?" he asked.

Well, duh! Of course I knew, and he knew I did. He was here two hours early last week to take dear Step-mama to the airport. I also knew that was the day Stella told him she couldn't stand his possessiveness and wouldn't go out with him anymore.

Hugh had sat silently at the kitchen table with me. Stella'd left making up her special tanning glop until that morning. We watched her carefully slide iodine into a pot that held hot baby oil. The sudden acrid smell had attacked my nose and made my eyes water. Stella bragged on her compound; how soft her skin felt, how she was going to get a tan to die for, and how great her new aqua strapless dress would look with her blonde hair and deep tan.

She always made the tanning solution herself, and recently improved on it by adding strongly brewed tea after it cooled to cut the iodine smell. A glass Pyrex measuring cup of tea stood waiting beside another filled with one of her concoctions. Stella fancied herself a "good witch" and messed around with herbs and homemade remedies. I also considered her a witch, the one with the green face, and I was Dorothy.

I filled a yellow legal tablet with Stella's dictation—where to reach her on which day, what magazines to cancel, yadda, yadda, yadda.

"I want you to use this on the vegetables instead of that commercial control," she said. "You only need to spray once a month."

She slapped my arm when I reached for the glass container next to the tea. "Don't do that, stupid, that's pure nicotine. You'll get ill if you get it on your hands. Use those gloves over there to fill the sprayer. Then let the cup sit with soap and water before you put it in the dishwasher. Do not forget to use the gloves. I don't want Hugh calling me home because you've got a tummy ache."

What a slam! The only time Hugh ever called her about me was when she was in the Greek Islands last year; I needed an emergency appendectomy and she had to fax her approval of the expenditure.

Before I could unclench my jaw and make some remark that would probably cause another big reduction in my allowance, Stella left the room.

Hugh stood up and walked over to look out the far kitchen window. I put a few dishes in the washer, checked out the refrigerator for perishables, and left to get the sprayer. Must be nice, I mused, to dump a guy and still have him around to take you to the airport. I substituted Brad Pitt for Hugh Dearing and dreamed on.

I returned to the kitchen with the sprayer and proceeded to fill the canister. Hugh watched, taking in every detail so he could tattle to the s-mom later. I snapped on the rubber gloves, unscrewed the sprayer cap, and slowly poured the brown liquid into the can. I picked up the sprayer in my right hand and waggled a good-bye to Hugh with my left. Hugh had evidently forgotten how to speak, so I mentally flipped him off. I was really glad I'd be rid of the two of them for a few weeks.

But it's only been six days now.

"Er, I'm afraid I have some bad news," he said. "Stella is dead."

I didn't move.

"The Mexican authorities are a little vague about the cause of death."

It seems that because of the weather, Stella couldn't sunbathe until two days ago. She took herself off to a deserted cove some distance from the hotel. The bad weather returned that evening, but not Stella. When the storm let up they found her on the cove's beach, but all her things had been swept out to sea. The hotel doctor thought perhaps her heart was not good, poor lady, or maybe an allergic reaction to something she ate. Hugh had made arrangements to have the body buried there.

He told me that Stella's death negated my guardianship and I would now come into my full inheritance.

I nodded my acknowledgment. Hugh stood up, put his hand down on my shoulder, and said I could call on him anytime; perhaps we could do dinner. I stayed mum. He squeezed my shoulder and left.

I sat on the porch a long time and thought about how Hugh was alone in the kitchen that day. I shivered. Maybe it could never be proved murder, but first thing tomorrow morning I'm having all the locks changed, hiring a new lawyer, and using only tanning lotions that come to me factory-sealed.

I returned to the garden and picked up my sprayer and a stick. "Yo, worm!" I called. "You want your dose of tea with one lump or two?"

~

# Rita's Revenge

CORA J. RAMOS

"What would you say if I told you someone was following us?" Rita whispered in his ear.

Pablo looked back down the road. There were no headlights. He pulled back the handles of his Harley and gunned the motor, trying to drown out the sound of her voice. The bike skidded forward as he eased off the clutch and sped toward the falls at Bass Lake. He had to get to the water, cool down, clear his head. It all happened so fast.

"It's not over." Rita's voice was louder now. "I'll have my way."

He tried to shut it out. He could almost feel her body squirm with delight. Once again she taunted him—after he'd thought it was over, that he'd showed her he was the one in control.

Ten years earlier, in high school, he'd had that charm that drove women wild. Rita had been the object of his unmerciful teasing then—by him and his friends. She was homely, gangly, and awkward and he'd played with her because he could. He strung her along, used her, broke her heart, then discarded her. She'd gone away and he'd forgotten about her, like the dozens of others. Then last month she'd showed up again. She'd become a real beauty—but with a vengeance.

That first day back, she'd walked into Nachos and found him and the guys. She'd thrown out that sexual vibe that was "muy malo"—that warned she could drive men to do things they'd never do if they stopped to think.

"I'm going to even the score with all of you," she threatened. "Mark my words. I'm going to have the last laugh in this town." She looked at Pablo and smiled seductively before turning and walking out without another word.

They all laughed. She couldn't hurt them.

But Hollywood had changed her. She'd become a very good actress. They could see how good she was when she started on Johnny, the weakest. Then one by one she went through all of them, making them believe she wanted them, needed them— that they could have her, that each was different from the rest. She had them almost salivating, believing they could stay in control and still have her. She broke each one, leaving them messed up big-time. Pablo knew she planned to start on him next—work him with her beauty and sex. She'd saved him for last and thought she was going to have her revenge, but he had devised his own plan to show her who was in control.

Tonight he'd swaggered into the Rainbow Ballroom ready for action on this night as sweltering and humid as it can be only in the San Joaquin Valley. He knew she'd be there because it was where he went every Friday night and he knew she'd be looking for him. He wore a one-size-too-small white tank top that accented his moist, glistening skin on his tanned muscles and upper torso, leaving it to a woman's imagination what lay hidden beneath the loose khakis below.

When he spotted Rita standing by the bar, wearing that low-slung red dress, he grew hard. He'd strutted up to her, gave her his most sexy look, and pulled her to him.

"You're dancing with me tonight."

He told her—didn't ask, didn't beg, didn't plead. Wasn't going to give her what she was asking for. Not then, anyhow. He would make her hot first. How could she resist? He knew she wanted him. All the women did.

He'd pressed her to him with his left hand as the music softened their bodies and danced her to the darkest corner. After a while, he pulled her hand to his chest and slid his right hand down her thigh. He slowly moved his hand up, lifting her skirt slightly and pausing suggestively before continuing over her waist, trailing his fingers up her bare back, then threading them through her hair. He pulled her head back forcefully, looked into her eyes without smiling, while brushing his lips lightly over hers.

She tried to turn into his kiss, but he pushed her head next to his and whispered into her ear, "You want me, don't you?" He felt her nod. He released her hair and slipped his right hand into his pocket.

He drew her closer, letting the Latin rhythms of the dance excite her. Slowly, he slid his hand up out of his pocket and pushed hard. She stiffened, then melted into him....

"I don't like it here. You used to take all the girls here. You know you'll have to pay for that."

She laughed, but it no longer mattered. The waterfall was just ahead and it would drown out her voice. The bike skidded to a stop. Pablo jumped off and headed for the falls. It wouldn't be long—escape the heat in the cool water—escape her voice.

"You can't escape, Pablo," she warned. "You started down this path years ago and I'm finishing it. I'll have my revenge."

Pablo ran faster to get away from the taunting, sliding in the muddy ruts from the splashing water. The falls were louder now, drowning her voice out of his head. Soon he could cool down in its spray.

He'd killed her there on the dance floor, slipping the switchblade out of his pocket and into her heart. Her red dress had been the perfect camouflage. Then he'd set her down on the bench in that dark corner, leaning her against the fake tree as the life ebbed from her body.

"You can't kill me, Pablito. I will be here in your head forever, taunting you and making you pay."

Her laughter grew louder. As he headed down to the falls he tripped over a tree stump. He couldn't stop the slide—couldn't catch himself. He grabbed for branches but everything eluded his grasp.

He slid uncontrollably over the edge, with Rita's laughter still ringing in his ears.

~

# Too Hot for Hanging

SUNNY FRAZIER

The temperature topped 112 degrees the day Cullie Cooper died in Theo Kearney's vineyard.

The only witnesses to Cullie's untimely demise were the Armenian field hands, fresh off the train and barely speaking English. One of their own did the killing, that much they agreed on. As they told it, Cullie's last act on earth was to cuss out a worker who riled the overseer worse than the rest. Cullie took the first swing and the two went down between the rows of grapes, dust flying. Only the Armenian got back up.

Someone from the estate had to ride into Fresno and fetch the law, but it was hot, and it was generally decided that Cullie couldn't get any deader. The messenger waited until the shadows were long before mounting a horse and following the row of palm trees leading to town.

Sheriff John Hensley had left that morning on a train bound for Sacramento, so it was Deputy Roland Tompkins who drove the wagon to the Kearney Estate. He examined the crime scene in the fading light. A grape stake with blood on the tip was the likely murder weapon. Tompkins ordered it ripped from the ground and placed in the wagon, along with the securely trussed foreigner and the remains of Cullie.

Although night covered the transport of the prisoner, word spread through Fresno faster than a lick of lightning. Cullie was not a town favorite, known only as a bully, a braggart, and a cheat at poker. But the citizens of Fresno distrusted even more the Armenians pouring into the county. Never mind that the newcomers suffered the heat without complaining while they picked melons, grapes, and everything else growing in the Great Valley. They dressed funny and talked different. They weren't to be trusted.

And now one of them had killed a citizen of Fresno.

By noon, Deputy Tompkins knew he had a situation on his hands. As the white-hot sun blazed down on the dusty streets, it raised the indignation of the town's ten thousand citizens to a feverish pitch. They gathered in front of the jail and called for Sheriff Hensley.

Tompkins peered through the window at the crowd. He spied a rope already tied in a noose and being waved above the heads. It was a lynch mob, all right. Didn't folks know the uncivilized West was a thing of the past? Now in 1889, hangings were conducted in an orderly manner. Except in Clovis, of course.

The deputy was willing to sit in the saddle while the sheriff was out of town, but could he hold tight to the reins if a riot broke out? He took stock of the five deputies under his charge. They seemed of a mind to hand the Armenian over if things got ugly. Tompkins hoisted his holster and felt the two Colts settle comfortably on his hips. He took a deep breath before stepping out to face the crowd.

"Hang the foreigner!" a barrage of voices greeted him.

Tompkins raised his hands to quell their cries. "Folks, I want to see this scoundrel hanged as badly as you do."

"Then hand him over!" shouted one of Cullie's drinking cronies.

"I'd oblige, but Sheriff Hensley is out of town. I reckon he's gonna insist on a fair trial."

"The man's guilty!" The crowd took up the chant and pressed forward.

50

Tompkins knew he would lose his badge if the sheriff came back and found a lynching had occurred in his absence. The deputy loved above all else the brass star worn proudly over his breast. He shined it daily until it reflected the gleam of justice to the citizenry he'd sworn to protect and serve. Now he had to protect them from their own hostility.

"You're right," he declared. "We surely should string this varmint up. Hand me the noose."

The rope was passed hand-over-head until it reached the jailhouse steps. When it was in his hands, Tompkins said, "You'll get your hanging. But not until the weather cools."

There were shouts of protest, but Tompkins cut them off. "No sir. It's too damn hot to hang the devil himself. I can't have you good people pressin' in close to get a good look at the rope cuttin' into the fella's neck, to see his tongue hangin' out and watch for his feet to twitch. Why, the ladies will faint with heat exhaustion."

It sounded reasonable. "When do we get to hang him?" someone asked.

Deputy Tompkins appeared to think on this. "I figure a hundred-and-one degrees is cool enough for you folks to withstand a decent hanging."

Once inside the jail, Tompkins barred the door and told a junior deputy, "Go fetch Doc Meux. Tell him we need an autopsy before Cullie gets too ripe."

Dr. Meux drove to the back entrance of the jail and parked his trap in the spare shade of an oak. Five days of heat wave had taken its toll on both the town and his own stamina. Folks were dropping like horseflies, collapsing with sun fever and heat exhaustion. Despite his instructions, women refused to loosen their corsets and their husbands worked outdoors at high noon. The doctor wrapped salted ice in towels and applied it to feverish foreheads, prescribed the extra consumption of water and recommended more leisurely activity during the hottest stages of summer. But, after two years, he was still a newcomer to Fresno and his advice was suspect.

Dr. Meux had already heard about the death of Cullie and anticipated the sheriff's call. The autopsy would be a relief from the relentless heat. At least it would be cool in the ice house where the body was kept.

Driving into town, he'd noted the crowd that lingered around the jail. The noose on the front desk told him the rest of the story.

He nodded to Tompkins and glanced at the prisoner in the cell. Dark eyes stared back. Intelligent eyes. They did not plead for mercy.

Entering the makeshift morgue, the smell of decay was evident. But then, Meux noted, Cullie Cooper was rotten inside and out well before his death. The doctor looked down upon the body stretched out on the slab of granite. There would be fewer calls for his services out at Kearney's estate, less need for the salves he applied and broken bones he set in the aftermath of Cullie's temper.

"Where does hate reside in a man?" Meux pondered aloud as he turned the body over. He probed the skull where dried blood matted over dark hair. Satisfied, he went outside to the pump and washed his hands.

"You done with Cullie?" Tompkins asked, as the doctor returned to the front desk.

"Yes. And I suggest you get him buried quickly and without ceremony before the stench makes everyone in the building sick." He handed Tompkins the death certificate.

The deputy looked up, puzzled. "Natural causes?"

"Cullie Cooper died of heat stroke." Dr. Meux picked up his medical valise.

"I don't want to tell you how to do your doctoring, but Cullie has a hole in the back of his head and I have a grape stake covered with blood in the wagon."

"The man fell on it when he collapsed."

Tompkins looked around to make sure the others weren't listening. "Doc, his own people saw the Armenian fella fighting Cullie."

"Did they see him actually kill Cullie?"

"Well, no. The two kinda fell to the ground on top of one another."

Dr. Meux, with all of the authority his position allowed, looked the deputy in the eye and said, "Cullie was killed by the sun and his own temper. His blood got so hot, it made him pass out and fall against the stake."

Tompkins scratched his head. "I don't know, Doc. Folks kinda had their hearts set on a hanging."

"Then it's your job to remind them Fresno is not a frontier town any longer. Release the prisoner and I will transport him back to the Kearney estate."

The townspeople received the verdict of natural causes better than expected, for they were self-righteous more than bloodthirsty. They were also drained by the heat and sought a facesaving solution to disperse. The prisoner was removed from the jail and spirited away in Dr. Meux's buggy.

The ride back to Kearney was hot and dusty. The men rode in silence as they passed the tall palms and brittle eucalyptus. Nearing their destination, Meux finally asked, "How much English do you understand?"

"I understand. I speak some."

"I've seen you on Butler Avenue, near the tracks. Folks call it Armenia Town."

The man stayed silent.

"I go there to treat your people. I know you. You heal people, too. Were you a doctor in your country?"

"I was a doctor. Yes."

Dr. Meux squinted as he looked down the road. "Then I guess we both know Cullie Cooper did not die of heat stroke."

"But you tell the deputy...."

The doctor cut him off. "I know what I said. And I also know the truth."

Kearney's mansion came into view. Dr. Meux reined the horses to a stop in front of the entry to the grounds. The man climbed out.

"Why do you lie for me?"

Meux searched the man's face. "I don't know if Cullie deserved to die, but I suspect he had it coming for a long time. You have the training and skills to keep people alive, and I could surely use the help. Weighed in the balance, your life needed to be spared for the very folks who wanted to hang you."

The man stood in the road as the doctor turned the buggy around and pointed the horses back toward town. Meux bent over to hand out one last piece of advice.

"Don't go thinking badly of Fresno just because of people like Cullie and the lynch crowd today. A city takes time to grow into itself. We need new blood." He sat up straight in the carriage seat. "But don't go bashing in any more heads, either. I can't get you off a murder charge a second time."

With that advice, Dr. Meux headed home. Justice, of a sort, was served.

~

*a Pool here*

# Fresno Heat

JO ANNE LUCAS

They call it Nells' Hell, this large ranch-style house that squats
by itself on the top of a dry, parched hill. Harold Nells had fall-
en for a king-of-the-mountain conceit and bought it in December from a bankrupt appliance dealer. Too bad he hadn't waited
for the warm months to show up its fatal flaw—the hill was hot
and unforgiving. The only green foliage to make a stand against
the heat was a few cowering shrubs that faced the northeast,
backed tight against the house, leaves and branches tucked pro-
tectively under the roofline.

It was Fresno in August and the air felt used, like it did when
you were a kid and you kept your head covered with a blanket
too long. To top it off, the household's air conditioning went on
the fritz. José, the Hispanic servant, slowly cleared away our dessert dishes and we moved to the library for after-dinner drinks.

I was the coolest dressed. I had on a skimpy little cocktail
number, barely legal on the streets, for my first meeting with
Harold Nells, and Larry trolled me like a feathered lure to attract
the stocky land developer's interest. Larry'd even brought several bottles of Tattinger's to grease the hook. Nells swallowed the
champagne, smacked his lips at me a few times, but didn't commit to the fancy business package Larry kept dangling.

Late evening and it was still hot. The chilled champagne felt
good going down. Doc Jamieson remonstrated with Nells for

drinking so much of the wine, but Nells bragged he would eat and drink anything now since Doc had changed his diabetes medicine. Doc cautioned him to moderation.

"Hell, Doc, if I was a moderate S.O.B., I'd still be bagging groceries in some two-bit store. Look around here, you don't get it this good 'less you're willing to grab at it all. Isn't that right, sweet cakes?" Nells patted my rear. I smiled at him over the rim of my champagne flute.

Larry laughed on cue. "Nells is no shy, retiring public servant like...what was his name?" Larry snapped his fingers at us. "That guy last year, the city councilman...Tarnally, yeah, Edward Tarnally. Remember him?"

"That sorry wimp," Nells growled. "Found he was finally playing hardball with real men and went off and killed himself after the first pitch."

I fed him the rest of my champagne; he rewarded me with a wet kiss.

"And you were the pitcher, I suppose?" I asked and slowly stroked his shoulders.

"Damn right, babe."

I looked up at him from under my lashes. "What kind of curve did you throw him?"

"Yes, Nells," Doc said, "I've always wondered, just exactly how did you get Tarnally to flip-flop his vote on your Westing Project?"

"Easy, I found out his pathetic little secret and asked if he was planning on being in the Vets' Parade again."

*Edward Tarnally had been a quiet and modest man who devoted his life to working for the public good. He volunteered hours each week at schools and hospices, worked unceasingly for land use reforms, and every year he marched in the Veterans' Day Parade, wearing a business suit and his row of medals earned for valor. Said he only wore the ribbons to honor those soldiers fallen in battle. And last year Edward Tarnally had shot himself the day after the parade.*

~

"I don't get it," I said. "What does marching in a parade have to do with selling you his vote?"

Nells laughed until he choked. "That sorry slob never saw any action. He was just a company clerk stationed in Virginia. Bought those fancy ribbons so's he could puff out his chest and feel like a man. I told him he could keep his medals long's he voted my way."

"So he voted for your Westing Project and killed himself," Larry said. "Wonder why he didn't leave a note, most suicides do."

"He did, he sent it to me. Said after the vote he couldn't stand himself and was taking the back door out. Reminded me of my promise not to tell."

"But, you just did," I said.

He shrugged. "Promises to dead men don't count." He knocked back the rest of the champagne.

Larry left the room for a call of nature, Doc brooded by the window, and Nells looked sleepy. I moved over by Doc and inclined my head toward Nells. Doc studied him and nodded.

When Larry returned we made motions to leave. Nells protested that it was still early. He and I walked outside with our arms around each others' waists. I said I'd drive back to see him after Larry dropped me off at my car. I suggested he do something to perk up and get ready for me, like take a swim.

"I'll wait for you in the pool, sweet cakes. Don't bother with no swimsuit." ~~his undoing~~

"I won't," I promised.

The servants were gone. We let ourselves out. Doc stayed behind in the driveway. Larry drove us down to a stand of eucalyptus trees at the base of the hill. I could hear the hum of the automatic air conditioner in my parked van. Larry unlocked the door and slid into the van's passenger seat. He greeted the dogs in back. I slipped out of my dress and heels and into a light-weight black jumpsuit and canvas shoes. I let the two German shepherds out for a break.

Larry consulted his watch and announced it was time. I secured the dogs in back and drove up the hill. Doc met us outside the front gate and we all walked around to the backyard. I called out a greeting as I slipped the leashes off the dogs. A splash and an unintelligible mumble answered me.

Harold Nells treaded water and held onto the pool's side with one hand. He shook his head as though to clear his vision.

"Hey, babe," he slurred, "what the hell?"

"I just slipped into my working clothes," I answered.

"Don' get it."

"Don't worry, 'babe,' you will." I gave a sharp command in German and the dogs took up positions on either side of the pool. Samson rushed at Nells, growling and snapping as if he would attack. Nells pulled his hand away from the coping. He swam for the other side. Herc lowered his ears and warned him away. Nells tried for the shallow end, but the dogs kept pace with him. The man's movements became more slow and heavy, even as he panicked. He tried to yell once, but swallowed water.

I stood by and watched the maneuvers. A car door slammed out front and a man joined me.

"Pete, what are you doing here?" I asked.

"Just getting the lay of the land for when I'm called in the morning," he replied.

I nodded. Nells barely moved now. Doc and Larry came out of the house. Larry said he put the original temperature control back on the air conditioner inside. "Whew! Never want to spend another evening in a sweat box like that again."

I asked him how he got rid of the servants. "Easy, I called them on the kitchen phone from my car earlier and tipped them that the Border Patrol was making a sweep of the area."

"Neat and tidy," I said.

"Mmmmm," he answered.

Doc said he'd removed Nells' new pills and left one of his expired prescription bottles in the medicine cabinet. The fact that Nells was taking placebos instead of insulin, along with the amount of wine, should send him into a diabetic coma soon. The dogs were on hand to keep him in the pool long enough for Nells to drift off to sleep and drown. Blood tests on the body would show Nells had a high level of alcohol in his system. It's always a tragic mistake to swim alone.

Pete, the newcomer, suggested we throw an air mattress in the pool to make it look like Nells fell asleep on it, rolled off, and was too drunk to swim.

"Good idea," Larry said. "How much longer do you think, Doc?"

Nells had stopped moving and was slowly sinking in the water.

"Not long," Doc answered.

I called the dogs while the men set the scene. We gathered by the pool's edge for one last look.

*You should always keep your promises to dead men,* I thought.

Pete wiped his forehead. "Man, this heat can sure get to you."

"Once in a while, son, justice needs some heat," Larry said. "You all ready for the wife beater at next week's little fishing drama up at the lake?"

"Yeah, I've been waiting a long time for him," Pete said. "Well, I'm off. See you back here in the morning after I discover the body, Doc."

One by one we left:

Deputy Peter Brazier, Fresno County Sheriff's Department;
Dr. MacCarthy Jamison, Chief-deputy Coroner, Fresno County;
Lawrence Hall, Assistant District Attorney, Fresno County;
Officer Candy Anderson, Fresno Police Canine Unit.
*FRESNO HEAT*

~

# Salt of the Earth

CORA J. RAMOS

The cooing doves awakened me gently to dawn on Saturday morning. Their thrumming massaged my spirit, fortifying me for the day ahead. I stared through the stems of the potted geraniums sitting on the windowsill at the blue sky beyond and felt like I'd never left.

I threw off the sheet, and that prickly sense of the heat to come hit me. No doubt about it, a sizzling day in the San Joaquin Valley lay ahead. Arriving late the previous night, I'd been rewarded with one of those cool, beautiful evenings that teased me to forget why I'd escaped to Los Angeles five years earlier; evenings that almost made up for the hot days. Almost.

I'd grown up in this house with Grams and Grandpa. How I would miss him. How she must miss him. Grams had kept her emotions buried since he'd died. I feared it would all hit her today at the memorial service. If she broke down, I had resolved to be strong for her.

After showering and putting on a cool shift, I headed down to the kitchen. I stood next to the doorway a moment before going in, listening to the soft whistling, and the ping of a wedding ring on the dishes as Grandma washed them.

"Morning, Grams."

"Well, darling, I thought you'd sleep longer than this. You

got in so late." She wiped her hands on the dishtowel and came over to give me a big hug.

"Sit yourself down and have some breakfast. Fixed your favorite home fries and vegetable omelet." She beamed to see me smile, then opened the oven door and pulled out some home-baked muffins. I was suddenly famished.

As the gift buyer for Magnis and Company on Rodeo Drive in Beverly Hills, I traveled and ate out often, with little time or energy for home cooking. I devoured everything on my plate and soaked up the emotional nourishment Grams bestowed on me. I tried not to feel guilty for thinking of food instead of Grandpa's death. But I knew encouraging the nurturing side of Grams helped her cope. It kept her mind off his death a little longer and we both benefited.

"I know your grandfather would be very pleased at this newly found appetite of yours. You always ate so little when you were home. Hurry and finish so I can show you the greenhouse. I've been growing some new varieties of flowers and I want you to tell me what you think."

Grandpa's pride had been his greenhouse. He'd spent most of his days propagating new varieties of all kinds of plants and flowers. His greatest joy was giving away cuttings and seedlings he'd nurtured and grown himself.

"I've been carrying on what he began." She opened the greenhouse door and let me go in.

After showing me her recent plantings and pinching a dead leaf here, pruning a small plant there, she stopped and sighed.

"What are you going to do with his ashes?" I asked.

There'd been no funeral service or burial when he'd died in Canada. I figured she had brought his ashes back and planned to bury him under one of his rose bushes he so prized, or maybe a new tree she'd plant in remembrance. Lots of people like having their loved ones near them, turning into some flower or tree— the desire to have life continue in some form.

"No, dear." She looked up at me with a comforting smile, as if it were harder for me to talk about him than it was for her. "I had his ashes strewn over the ocean that he loved so much."

"I never knew he loved the ocean. He never mentioned it. Why did you both choose to live here in the valley, then?"

"He did it for me. I couldn't bear being away from my family. He soon found he liked growing things, so what better place? He came to love it here but he never lost that special place in his heart for the ocean. Don't you remember how all our vacations were somewhere at the coast—Pismo, Monterey, Carmel? Even when we visited Mexico it was near the ocean."

I nodded, remembering. But the smell of the humid, moist earth wafted through the windows, filling me with memories of days by Grandpa's side working in the earth. "I'm amazed you've managed to keep the greenhouse in such good shape. Who's helping you? I know you couldn't do all this by yourself. I haven't forgotten how much goes into it."

"Well, it has been difficult, but our neighbor Charlie's fifteen-year-old grandson comes over on Fridays to help me in here. I do all the potting myself and he just cleans and waters some."

"He takes care of the compost pile, too?"

"Oh, I take care of that. The gardener empties the grass clippings on it when he comes every two weeks. I add bone meal and lime and keep it moist. The heat does the rest. I don't have to turn it—it decomposes quickly enough. I started a second one so that I could let the old one just sit for the year without much work. When I need soil, I simply dig out from the bottom where it's nice and soft and light. It works out."

She gave me a reassuring smile and seemed genuinely happy.

"I've come to enjoy working in the greenhouse since I've taken it over. I now understand why your grandpa enjoyed it all those years—the ongoing life in there. Gives one such a sense of peace and comfort."

That night, after the memorial service and the afternoon potluck the neighbors had organized, we sat on the porch talking. The day had gone smoothly and Grams had been a gracious hostess, smiling and upbeat. I'd just begun getting nostalgic about how nice the summer evenings could be, when I was reminded again why I'd left. As the evening advanced, all breezes gradually withered and the heat surrounded us like a blanket you couldn't throw off.

Since Grams had no air conditioning and didn't want it, there was only a swamp cooler downstairs. Upstairs, we were left to the mercy of portable fans in the bedrooms. I got them out of the attic and set them up on tables near the open windows, hoping to pull in any coolness the night might deign to offer us. We ended up in the living room next to the swamp cooler, talking into the early morning hours, reminiscing about Grandpa and their life together. I figured I would be lucky to have a love like theirs someday.

Sunday burned hot from early on. It never let up and all I wanted to do was lie in the hammock under the oak tree and drink Gram's limeade.

Monday morning came as Saturday had, the precursor of yet another hot summer day. I consoled myself, knowing I'd be in my air conditioned car and out of the Valley before noon.

"You're lucky," Grams smiled as she set out the toast and filled our coffee cups at breakfast. "At least it will only be in the low one-hundreds."

I laughed, knowing she meant it wouldn't go over one hundred and ten, today at least. "This heat is good for only one thing."

"What's that?" She played along.

"Well, it's good for the compost pile."

We had a good laugh. It was a joke Gramps had always made when I complained about the hot weather.

I remembered the day I'd left to make a life for myself in Los Angeles. He was running his fingers through the soil. "Good

63

stock you come from, girl, grounded like this salt of the earth. I don't worry about you, Nina. You've felt the earth, dug your fingers into it, worked it, watered it, and seen it produce abundance. You'll always put down roots wherever you go. You'll never feel like a ship at sea, thrashed about and unable to control your destiny." The sun reflected off his gold tooth as he smiled. Those words came back to me whenever I was tempted to feel sorry for myself. I knew I would always make it because of what he taught me in the greenhouse.

Grams smiled as if she'd remembered some intimacy they'd shared. It relieved me to know her sense of humor was intact and her spirits were up. I didn't feel so guilty about having to return to Los Angeles. I'd rest easy knowing she'd be fine.

Two years earlier, just after Grandpa's first stroke, I'd been home on a visit and had gotten up about midnight, unable to sleep. I'd come down the back kitchen stairs and heard them talking. Their conversation had that intimate tone and I didn't want to intrude. As I turned to go back upstairs, I heard Grandpa saying, "Elsie, promise me. You have to—that's what I want. If it ever comes down to it, I want to be here with you and my beloved plants." I had assumed he'd wanted to be cremated and buried on the property.

Six months later, Grams called again and said Grandpa had had a second stroke and fallen very ill. She called again and informed me that she'd taken him to Canada where she'd found a clinic that would be able to treat him and maybe cure him. She corresponded from Canada for the first three months, saying he was improving. Then she returned home to take care of business, while he stayed there for his treatment.

Last month she'd called and said he'd had a sudden turn for the worst and had died. She told me she was going back for his ashes. The next time I talked with her she said she found out from the nurses that he'd been dreaming of the ocean and wanted to go there one more time.

I guess that's what made her decide to scatter his ashes in the ocean up there instead of bringing them back here. She fulfilled the desire he'd had when they were first married.

I drove off to L.A. later that morning, with the pot of geraniums Grams had picked from the greenhouse especially for me. The question of why she hadn't stayed with Gramps in Canada had been answered without having had to ask. She obviously felt compelled to maintain his beloved greenhouse for him until he was back home again—only he never got back home.

When I finally reached L.A., I left my luggage in the car, deciding to unload it later. I felt tired and needed to lie down. The whole trip had drained me more than I realized. I grabbed my purse, the pot of geraniums, and the bag of cookies Grams had baked and went into my courtyard apartment. As I closed the door, the tears came. Being at the house, nurtured by Grams, I hadn't felt the full impact of the loss. I missed him terribly.

I set everything down on the coffee table, reached for a tissue to wipe away my tears, and my hand hit the pot of geraniums, sending it flying. I was dismayed to see it lying in pieces on the floor. When I checked, the plant wasn't too damaged, only a few broken leaves.

I went to retrieve an empty clay pot I'd stored under the sink a few months back and began scooping the dirt off the floor into the pot when I noticed something shiny mixed in the soil. I picked it up, thinking it was a piece of glass, but a chill ran down my spine as it slowly dawned on me. I slumped back against the couch. It was Grandpa's gold tooth.

I suddenly understood when I remembered the rest of the conversation I'd overheard that night. "Elsie, promise me. You have to—that's what I want. If it ever comes down to it, I want to be here with you and my beloved plants."

Grams had answered, "The city would never allow it. That's what graveyards are for."

Now it hit me. Gramps hadn't died in Canada. He'd never

even been there. Grams faked the letters to create a diversion and give her time. I sank down in a chair. I couldn't believe it. He'd died at home. He was where he wanted to be, near his beloved Elsie and his greenhouse—in the compost pile.

~

# ~STORMY WEATHER~

# Rain Checked

JO ANNE LUCAS

I'd first fallen in love with Vince Cabot when I was seven and he eleven. I shadowed him and my brother all summer and became their willing co-conspirator and often the scapegoat of their worst schemes. That part just killed me, but if Vince even crooked his dark eyebrow my way, I wiped my tears and jumped at the chance to do it all again. Then that September I saw Tom Cruise in *Top Gun* on TV and decided seven was too young for total commitment. I moved on.

Sometime after I turned twelve Vince and his family left the neighborhood, but he dropped by to visit my brother Sam at truly tacky times like when I was having a sleep-over and all of us girls wore mud packs and curlers, or when I'd just returned from a week of backpacking. Not what you'd want in your memory book. Eventually, he stopped coming by.

Last week I attended a party for the opening of a showing of medieval costumes at the museum and Vince Cabot plunged back into the waters of my life like the *Titanic* searching for an iceberg. He seemed slightly amused, in his Pierce Brosnan way, that I'd grown up. A wraith of that long-ago little girl whispered urgent warnings to me, but I was enthralled with this handsome dreamboat.

"Get lost, kid," I told the wraith and settled back to enjoy myself.

We made a date for lunch downtown. I was to meet him at the old Pacific Southwest Bank building where he had a business meeting with his rich Uncle Horace. Vince promised that it would only take ten minutes and then we would go eat at the ritzy Golden Frog Dining Palace.

The next morning I dressed carefully, hopped the bus, and rode straight into a cloudburst tantrum. What a deluge; I couldn't even make out the old bank's tall, green-tiled roof from the bus window, and me with no umbrella. Where was my fairy godmother when I needed her?

When the bus let me off, I scowled up at the rain and ran as fast as I could for the building's entrance. I was really dripping when Vince met me in the lobby. He said he'd just arrived, too. I caught our reflection in the glass revolving door. He looked impeccable—as elegant as a chilled martini, while I resembled a slopped-over brewski.

Embarrassed, I dripped my way into the first elevator. Good thing we had it to ourselves for Vince proceeded to kiss me in a way I've only read about.

"Wow," I silently told the ghost of my childhood, "this is even better than I dreamed."

The kid kept quiet.

I'd been thoroughly kissed and was panting when the elevator doors parted on the fifth floor; luckily everyone had left for lunch. Vince led me to his uncle's office and opened the door for me. The spacious room was deserted except for the dead man sprawled in the desk chair. He had a wicked-looking knife stuck in his chest.

Soon after I called 911, we had a cop crowd. Vince identified the corpse as his uncle, Horace Myers, and explained how we'd just arrived and discovered him.

In my mind the kid yelled at me, "You're being set up again."

I stared at his face; it wore that complacent look I well remembered. I veiled my eyes with my lashes and smiled up at him. He had miscalculated this time. Sure, he was a good kisser and all, but I'd never cover for a killer.

So I told the cute police detective that Vince had been as dry as a Fresno heat wave when we met downstairs. This proved he'd been inside the building long enough to commit the murder before I arrived. Also, as for motive, he had long ago told me he was his uncle's only heir.

The detective took in my wet shoes and hair, noted the time, then took Vince Cabot in for murder. He also took my phone number.

The kid gave me a thumbs-up.

When I stepped outside later, I leaned against one of the tall Corinthian columns of the old bank and thought about how some fairy godmothers came in amazing shapes these days. I tilted my head back and squinted up against the rain. "Hey, lady, way to go!"

Then I did the Gene Kelly bit on my way to the bus stop.

~

# Final Forecast

SUNNY FRAZIER

"Blame it on El Niño," my husband said as he packed his valise.

But I was more inclined to blame the storm clouds hanging over our marriage on Nina, the weather-girl-in-training at the Fresno television station where Doug worked as a meteorologist. I had no recourse but to watch the man slide out of my life like one of those hillside houses in San Francisco.

"Blame it on El Niño," I muttered as I made myself a cup of Earl Grey. When I reached for a packet of sugar substitute, it was empty. I checked the recently purchased box and found about half of the packets were defective. White powder spilled from the unsealed edges. It figured. Doug always insisted on shopping at grocery outlets for off-brands and foodstuffs well past the expiration date. Someday his cheapness would kill him. I started to throw the box in the garbage can, but changed my mind.

"Blame it on El Niño," my hairdresser, Manuel, consoled me when I told him of the impending divorce. "Being beautiful is the best revenge." He proceeded to cut and color my hair and I walked out a different woman. Even Doug wouldn't recognize me.

"Blame it on El Niño," said the man behind the counter at a hardware store in a distant town. "It brings the vermin out in droves. This should get rid of your problem." He handed me a box of rat poison. I threw it in my basket, along with glue and a package of latex gloves.

When Doug came over to pick up the rest of his things, I made coffee.

"I'm glad you're being adult about this," he told me as he emptied four packets of sweetener into his cup. "I've drawn up a settlement I think we can both live with."

"Blame it on El Niño," the driver said when the ambulance arrived thirty minutes later. The streets were flooded by heavy rains that Doug had accurately predicted in the last weathercast he would ever deliver.

There was an inquest into Doug's death, and I, of course, was found innocent. The story of the tampered sweetener made national news, and stock in the industry plummeted. I sued and walked away with fifteen million dollars, which was a great deal more than the chintzy alimony Doug planned to give me.

The weather went back to normal and life was sweet again.

Only one person was left out in the cold. But then, I blamed it on Nina all along.

~

# ~DEADLY DESTINATIONS~

# Arrest in Peace

SUNNY FRAZIER

The Fresno morgue is always cold, no matter what time of year, but in December the atmosphere seems chillier than usual. The walls close in and the awareness of surrounding death is as keen as the wind cutting through the trees outside.

On December 22, instead of shopping for Christmas presents like the rest of the world, I was studying the structure of the human skeleton, memorizing the names of all the bones and where they go in the Erector Set we call the human skeleton. I'd pulled Watch I corpse patrol, which was like being in solitary confinement with death.

At two A.M. the bell rang announcing visitors from the world of the living. I put a bookmark in the massive volume of *Gray's Anatomy* and hurried up the ramp to unlock the heavy doors.

"Hey, Lady Jane. Slow night for the meat wagon." Cob Turner's words were punctuated by clouds of white fog, as thick as the tule fog swirling around us. He rubbed his leather-gloved hands and stamped his feet before turning around to open the rear doors of the van.

Junior had the body bag on the gurney and was ready to give it the heave-ho. "Another one to add to your collection, Janie," he said somberly. Being Hispanic, Junior was just a little more reverential about the cargo than Cob.

I walked ahead, leading the men and the body to the holding rack in the corner of the room where it would keep me company all night. I offered the men coffee, a Blue Mountain blend from Jamaica, which was a much-needed indulgence to get me through the atmosphere and my studies.

"If business was dead, I'd commit murder just to drop by for your coffee," sighed Cob.

Junior walked over to the book and flipped it open to the marked page. "You studying the bones now?"

"I have to have them memorized by the end of semester break."

He laughed. "Yeah, I remember doing that. It's a lot of bones."

Cob started chanting, "Knee bone connected to the thigh bone. Thigh bone connected to the hip bone," until he was connecting bones in absurd ways that had Junior and me choking on our coffee.

Finally they left and I went back to my studies. I was humming the bone song when I first heard it. It was a soft whirring sound, like a kitten purring.

Any sound, other than those I might make, were suspect and had to be investigated. Unless, of course, it was all in my head. I waited and wondered if I imagined the whirring. But I didn't imagine the sharp "click."

It came from the latest body bag.

I stared at the black plastic and tried to imagine what was inside. I mean, I *knew* what was inside. I just didn't know what condition the corpse was in or what mechanical device was in there with him or her.

Knowing that I should go back to my studies and pretend I never heard any sounds, I still went for the zipper. The face was intact, no injuries there. In fact, he was ruggedly handsome, like the Marlboro Man. I continued slowly. The death blow was in back of the head. No blood on the shirt, no chest wounds. Nice chest. The zipper caught momentarily on the large belt buckle advertising Coors beer. Must be from Clovis, I decided. I tugged again at the zipper.

"Why did you want to meet me here?"

I jumped back in surprise. When I collected my senses and got my heartbeat to slow down, I went back to the belt buckle. It would be removed before John Doe was assigned a cold storage box, so I figured I'd help the process. Carefully I pulled the belt out of the loops and zipped the bag back up.

I examined the buckle under my study light. It was purposely large to disguise a micro-cassette recorder. Nearly as small as a cigarette lighter, it attached to the buckle with a few metal prongs. I could picture John Doe standing with his thumbs hooked behind the buckle, controlling the on-and-off switch.

The tape was evidence to the death (or murder) of Mr. Doe and I knew I should hand it over to the police. But how would I know if it was important enough to hand over to the authorities if I didn't listen to it first?

The dialogue went back and forth, the second man just a little harder to hear. It seemed to be an argument over drugs. The second man kept saying he had the "ice" in a safe place where nobody would look for it. John Doe said he wanted out, just hand over $10,000 and keep the drugs. Threats were tossed out and the second man got angrier and angrier.

Suddenly, I heard the first man yell, "No! No!" followed by sounds of something hard—a board or a baseball bat—connecting with bone. Screams of pain filled the morgue and I listened helplessly as bones cracked.

And in the background of the tape was another sound.

"Oh, the knee bone's connected to the thigh bone. The thigh bone's connected to the hip bone. The hip bone's connected...."

The killer was Cob.

I stared at the tiny recorder in my hand. Carefully, I turned it off.

"Hey Lady Jane, the coffee was so good tonight, I came back for a refill."

I swung around and saw Cob standing at the top of the

ramp. I thought I locked the door, but remembered he'd let Junior and himself out. I slipped my hand holding the tape recorder behind my back.

"You look like you've seen a ghost." He chucked me under the chin, but his eyes studied my face. "Guess it could happen in this place, right, sugar?"

The morgue felt small and cold, like a tomb. I was interred with seven corpses and a killer.

"Let me mark my place and then I'll get us both some coffee," I said in my most ingratiating voice. I walked over to the anatomy book and slipped the recorder down the spine of the book where constant use made it pull away from the binding.

I grabbed two Styrofoam cups and poured coffee, black for Cob and two sugars for me. When I turned, he had the Marlboro Man's body bag unzipped.

"What are you doing?"

"I coulda sworn there was a big ol' belt buckle on this boy when he came in," Cob drawled. "You didn't by chance remove it, did you, Janie?"

My eyes involuntarily darted to the table where I'd dropped the belt. The buckle was next to it. Cob walked over and picked them up.

"It's not like you to take souvenirs, Cob."

"I think there was more to this belt buckle. Why don't you hand it over." He started to approach me, his mouth clenched in a grin, his eyes hard as gravestones.

I threw both cups of scalding hot coffee in his face. Cob screamed and reached out blindly to grab me. I ducked and got around him and ran up the ramp.

Arms grabbed me. I fought wildly, then I heard Junior's voice saying, "Whoa, Janie. Where you headed in such a rush?"

Was Junior in on this, too?

"Whatcha doin' here, partner?" Cob asked.

"I came back to help her with the anatomy lesson." He stared at Cob's burned face and the puddle of coffee, then drew the wrong conclusion. "Did he try to come on to you, Jane?"

"He's a murderer. He's the one who killed your last delivery."

Cob came after me, but Junior hid me behind his muscular back.

"Is this true?" he asked Cob.

"Junior, who you gonna believe? Your partner or the morgue girl?"

Junior paused. "This is a big accusation. You got any evidence, Jane?"

"There was a tape recorder on the corpse. The whole murder was recorded. It's all the evidence the homicide detectives will need."

Junior believed my story. He drew a gun and trained it on Cob.

"What's that, a toy gun? You know we can't carry firearms, Junior."

"You can't, Cob, but I'm a with the Sheriff's Department. We've been following your drug trail for months, but I couldn't catch you at anything. So we sent in a confidential informant and I wound up carrying him off in a body bag. If Janie has the tape recorder we planted, then we're putting you away for a lifetime—which is longer than that poor bastard ever had."

Cob made a dash down the ramp and around the racks, heading for the back door. His shoulder hit a rack and the body bag of the CI tumbled out. Cob tripped over it and came down hard on the cement floor. The crack of his femur reverberated in the room.

"You have the right to remain silent," Junior read from his Miranda card while Cob screamed in pain.

His thigh bone wasn't connected to his hip bone anymore. And, I noted, he was singing a whole different tune.

~

# Jealous Jewels

JO ANNE LUCAS

Memories are the DNA of life. They become entombed in a treasury of faceted jewels: clear blue sapphires reflecting childhood joys; unflawed diamonds pledging pure love; lusty red rubies dripping revenge.

I love my rubies.

It was a foggy December night in Clovis, but that didn't diminish the size of the crowd at the popular Jim's Place. I'd been tipping my brandy into his rum and Coke, laughing at his corny quips, and promising all for over an hour. Keeping time to the country-western music, his confidence swelled in direct proportion to this handling. My eyes convinced him he was my knight in a shiny cheap suit, my lips swore testimony to his limp charm. Craig Null, aging office equipment salesman, came on like a swaggering Clint Eastwood, and I made like his Madison County Bridge waiting to happen.

We preferred the lounge's darkened corner to the crowds and lights at the horseshoe bar. Craig told of his failure to consummate an appointment with John L. Hendrickson earlier. The great John L. had kept him hostage for four hours in the lobby, then jilted him through the receptionist's professional smile. Craig'd heard how Hendrickson frequented this bar and decided to capture his prospect's interest over a drink.

I shook out another Virginia Slim. He quickly reached for my derringer-shaped lighter. "Let me," he said, and lit my cigarette.

I laughed. "You ought to do the same for this Mr. Hendrickson. It'd certainly grab his attention."

Null looked like he'd just had a bright idea. I fumbled with my purse and knocked the derringer to the floor. He picked it up and set it on the table. I caressed his cheek and left to visit the little girls' room.

From the pay phone down the short hallway I could see the bartender answer on the third ring. He sent a waitress to summon my party.

I watched and waited for a large and familiar figure to pick up the receiver, then I went into my apologetic overseas operator routine and crackled some cellophane near the mouthpiece. The impatient man pulled out a cigarette and patted his pockets for a light. My erstwhile knight rode up and brandished the lighter. The big man gave him a look of surprise that was instantly reflected by everyone else after Null pulled the trigger and shot John L. Hendrickson. Null couldn't believe what had happened and turned the barrel around to peer into it as he pulled the trigger again.

It was a straight case of murder and suicide in front of forty witnesses. I replaced the receiver and left by the fire exit.

I guess you could say John L. had taught me well; timing and guts are what it takes to stay ahead in the game. I added a twist of my own because I'd be damned if I was going to let him dump sixteen years of marriage for a twenty-something bimbo with more bust than brains.

So, here's to John L. Hendrickson, King of the Clichés:

Thanks for the memories.

Light 'em if you've got 'em.

Bang, you're dead.

~

# Hickory Dickory

SUNNY FRAZIER

Some people called her Dottie, some called her the Clock Lady and more than a few called her crazy. Dorothy didn't care. The only thing that mattered in life was time—and Dorothy had plenty of that on her hands.

Clocks were Dorothy's passion. Her love for timepieces grew from the time her father, a watch repairman, sat Dorothy on his lap as he worked. It wasn't long before her tiny fingers were helping him with the springs and wheels that made time pass. Soon she was creating her own clocks out of spare parts, bigger and more elaborate clocks than anyone could imagine. She didn't sell them, but instead decorated her front yard with her creations.

From the moment she woke up—precisely at 6:05—Dorothy made every minute of her day count. First she fed the cats, Tic and Toc. Then she went outside to sweep the driveway. Armed with rags and cleaners, she proceeded to wash dirty faces.

Clock faces. Big clocks, little clocks, all with dirty hands and faces. Dust from the street traffic seeped into the cracks, so every day Dorothy tidied up. And when she was done polishing, she opened the wide front gate to her yard and welcomed the world to her place in time.

Today there was someone waiting at the gate. An early visitor? The closer she got, the more familiar the figure became.

"Hi, Aunt Dot. Long time, no see."

Rupert leaned on the wrought-iron gate, filthy from the top of his sweatband to the tips of his Birkenstocks. He wore his hair long and his beard longer. The grin pasted on his face didn't fool her. She suspected her nephew was out of money and out of options. That's the only time he ever paid a visit.

"This is a surprise! What brings you to town, Rupert?" she asked.

"My girlfriend threw me out and my mom won't take me in." Rupert's whining and self-pity had grown old, even though he failed to mature. Dorothy sighed and took him in once again.

The first few days, Rupert ingratiated himself by helping out. He propped a ladder at the base of the Seth Thomas replica street clock and shined up all four faces. He weeded the flower bed so the numbers of the garden clock could be clearly seen. He fixed the cuckoo clock so the little wooden girl would ride up and down as the wheels of the clock turned. He even trimmed his beard, washed his hair, and charmed the tourists who took time out of their busy lives to look at the Clock Lady's display.

"You oughta start charging, Auntie," Rupert said one day. "Donations aren't enough to keep this place ticking."

Soon money became a constant subject of conversation. "How much is this place worth, Aunt Dottie?" Rupert badgered. He eyed the safe in the parlor and Dot found him sneaking a peek at the bank book in the credenza.

One night Dot was awakened out of a deep sleep. It wasn't the chiming of the clocks all over the house that woke her—she was used to that noise. No, it was the sound of Rupert talking to someone over the telephone. Dot tiptoed to the bedroom door to listen.

"I'm telling you, she's loaded. No, I don't know where she keeps it, but I'll keep looking. The old girl's crafty. But her time's running out."

Rupert hadn't changed one bit. Dot knew she had to protect

her valuables, and she had to do it in a timely manner. The clock was ticking.

The next day she got up early and made a racket as she fussed with the safe. She took out a small package and slipped it under her robe. Making no attempt to be quiet, Dot got the ladder out of the storage room and propped it up to the carillon tower. She leaned the ladder against the balustrade and climbed to the top, careful to avoid the flywheels and gears of the nineteenth-century German clock movement. The package slipped snugly inside the workings. As she climbed down the ladder, she saw a slight movement at the kitchen curtains.

That night Dottie forced herself to stay up past her bedtime. Rupert kept her company, punctuating his conversation with exaggerated yawns. He finally got up, stretched, and announced, "Time for bed. Are you turning in, Auntie?"

"In a minute. I think I'll have a cup of warm milk first."

Dottie took her time, heating the milk slowly on the stove instead of zapping it in the microwave. She skimmed off the skin, then poured some in Tic and Toc's bowls. At 11:40 she turned off the television, rinsed her cup, and made a commotion while preparing for bed.

Five minutes later, she heard footsteps down the hall and the squeaky hinge of the front door. Dot peeked out of her bedroom window. Rupert had the ladder braced against the carillon tower. In the light of the full moon, she watched him climb behind the pressed tin covering the main gears. His greed made him hasty.

At thirty seconds to midnight, Dot heard a triumphant cry. Rupert had obviously located the bag of valuables. She smiled sadly, thinking of her loss.

On the stroke of midnight, the carillon tower rang out the hour. The loud bong of the heavy chimes drowned out the screams. When the clock finished its twelfth strike, the screaming had stopped.

~

The next morning, the newspaper boy found Rupert's legs dangling from the clock tower and a pool of blood beneath. Soon police cars filled the courtyard. Dot stood in her housecoat, surveying the crime scene.

"Ma'am, we found this bag in what was left of your nephew's hands," the detective informed her. "Would you know anything about it?" He opened the bag and out spilled half a dozen antique pocket watches.

"They were my father's," Dottie said. "They haven't run in years. I wondered where they'd disappeared to."

"Did you know your nephew had a criminal history of theft?" the detective asked delicately.

"Oh, my goodness. Are you saying he planned to steal my precious timepieces?" Dot took a Kleenex and dabbed at her eyes.

"I'm afraid it looks that way," said the detective, shaking his head."Unfortunately, he picked a dangerous place to stash the bag. Although the neighbors say they haven't heard that particular clock chime in years."

"Yes, it's very strange. He must have unjammed the gears and triggered the chimes as he hid the bag."

Dot pretended to weep as they removed the body. Rupert had always been a handful. His criminal leanings were bound to catch up with him.

It was just a matter of time.

~

87

# The Butler in the Brine

J. A. LUCAS

Of course I didn't call the police. I was playing Harpo Marx, and you don't drop your dramatic persona just because someone gets killed. I am a professional, and the show must go on.

We were Comics on Call, working for two weeks at the Bass Lake Resort, doing our Mayhem & Marx bit. Everything had jelled nicely early on, and the vacation crowd ate up our act each time we appeared to commit our planned and extemporaneous maniac skits around them. Not only did we play off the audience well, but also Max Heller, the Las Vegas talent scout, was checking us out and he looked very, very interested.

The trouble was that John Snood forgot he was Jeeves the butler and not the romantic lead. He had taken to acting out some steamy love scenes behind the sets with the wife of a jealous guest. Our butler no longer stood in the wings waiting to serve. He now floated face down in deep water off the private pier.

I honked meaningfully at Groucho, but he had lost it. The old boy leaned against the boathouse, eyebrows and cigar drooping. Chico retched off-stage in some bushes, and tall Mrs. Worthy Bucks screamed a ragged high C without being pinched.

The scene had lost its focus.

I ad-libbed a few more honks and did my crazed and crafty shtick as I grappled for the boat hook. I feinted a few passes at Groucho and Mrs. WB, but they didn't pick up on my cues. Max Heller left. I leered at the audience still on hand and did an elaborate creep down the pier, peering from side to side in an exquisite pantomime of paranoia. Then I neatly caught Jeeves on my boat hook and dragged him out of the water from between two sporty Chris Crafts.

The corpse sprawled in a sodden mess at my feet. Someone had cracked his cranium with a wine bottle and little bits of green glass winked from the back of his head.

I mimed loving grief and slowly turned him over. From my inside coat pocket I pulled out my cherished rubber chicken and laid it in his arms.

Then I honked inconsolably into my red over-sized handkerchief and thought that if anyone could have killed our group's big chance with Max Heller in Vegas, *the butler did it.*

~

# Shudder Bug

SUNNY FRAZIER

We all had an image of Marta Ryan imprinted in our minds. She was the girl in high school who seemed to be looking ahead, past graduation and definitely beyond marriage and children. The Nikon camera around her neck signaled aspirations that could not be contained in a small town like Lemoore. As the class of '69 threw their mortarboards into the air, Marta threw hers into the ring. She headed for Los Angeles and never looked back.

But we heard about her. Her stark photographs of the Hollywood homeless appeared in *Life* magazine. The black and white prints were compared to Dorothea Lange and she was hailed as the next Margaret Bourke-White. Even more fascinating were the photographs of the artist. She was no longer "plain" Marta. The intensity was still there, but now she looked sophisticated.

When she came back to Lemoore and set up a small darkroom in an empty building off D Street, there was plenty of fanfare. I was surprised she even called to tell me she was home. We weren't close in high school, but we shared a love of photography. We were the only female shutterbugs in photography club.

I paid a visit to her studio and the smell of developer instantly took me back to a time of f-stops and ASA's. The red light was on over the darkroom door, so I knew Marta was inside working her magic. While I waited, I looked over her latest prints spread out on a drafting table.

"What do you think, Ginger?" She came up behind me, wiping her hands on a stained apron.

The San Joaquin Valley was her point of focus. Poppies growing in a junkyard, an old windmill in moonlight, starlings nesting under a bridge. Images I passed by everyday. She was working with color this time. I picked up a print and recognized the Depression-era store which stood across from Hall's Corner. "Live and let live" was scrawled across the doorless entry.

"They're going to bulldoze the old grocery next week," I commented.

"Good. I'll have the only print of it."

So much for nostalgia.

Marta was getting ready for yet another show. What made this one different was that she had come home to a town she swore she'd never set foot in again. The media billed her as "Valley Photographer Returns to Her Roots" and she played up the angle in every interview.

But those of us who had never left Lemoore were suspicious. The Marta we knew was like an iceberg, cold on the surface and treacherous under the waterline.

While Marta was making her meteoric rise to fame, I'd married, divorced, and now worked as a clerk in City Hall. I'd kept up my high school ties with Evan Smoldt and Bobby Menezes, reporters for the *Lemoore Advance*. I joined them at the Last Drop coffee shop on Main Street to compare notes.

"Why do you think she's come back?" I asked.

"We have a class reunion coming up," suggested Bobby.

Evan pushed back his fedora. Men under seventy didn't wear fedoras anymore, but Evan was full of affectations. "Well, she could be pining for days gone by." Bobby and I snickered. "Seriously though, I heard she's made contact with Mike Warrington."

We exchanged knowing glances.

Mike Warrington had been the quarterback for the

Lemoore Tigers. It was rumored that Marta had a crush on him but he could have any girl—why bother with plain Marta? When he blew out his knee at the homecoming game, it shattered his dreams of playing college ball. Mike married the homecoming queen, never went to college, and now worked at the local dairy making cottage cheese.

Bobby went into reporter mode. "Why don't you pay her a visit and find out what's up?"

When I entered Marta's studio I found her in the small room she used as sleeping quarters. She was bent over a camera on a tripod low to the floor.

"What are you photographing down there? Dust?"

"I'm doing a little time-lapse photography. I found a black widow in the corner and I'm going to record it spinning its web. One frame per hour. I may do a series around it."

A black widow. How appropriate, I thought.

"Word on the streets is that you got in touch with Mike."

She shot me a warning look. "Nothing's changed in this town, has it? Everyone's in everybody's business." She pulled out an unfiltered cigarette and lit up. "Yeah, I looked Mike up. He hasn't done too well since high school."

"A steady job, a family—I'd say he's done about average."

She blew a wreath of smoke. "Mike always wanted fame and fortune. Looks like he missed out on both counts. I think he's ready for a change."

Her smile had all the venom of her pet project in the corner.

"You're going to make him an offer he can't refuse?" I ventured to guess.

"I wanted him back in high school. Now I've got something he wants." She went back to adjusting the Nikon.

"It would be hard to be discreet," I warned.

"I don't plan on being discreet." She snubbed the cigarette out in an empty film canister. "Not that it's any of your business, but I've already propositioned him and he's already accepted. And none of this slip-in and slip-out. He's going to stay the whole night tonight. I've got something his wife can't give him—money and fame."

I was too disgusted to listen to more. Unfortunately, Marta had Mike pegged right. Something in him hungered for the limelight, even if it meant riding on someone else's shoulders. I stopped by the *Advance* and told Bobby and Evan her plan.

"I never trusted her," Bobby said with disgust. "Maybe somebody should talk sense into Mike before it's too late."

"Maybe someone should warn his wife," said Evan.

"Or maybe somebody should stop her," I said. They nodded in agreement.

I was doing my morning jog down D Street when I saw an ambulance and two of the three police cars the city owned parked in front of Marta's studio. As I pulled up to the scene, two paramedics pushed a gurney out of the studio door. There was a draped figure on it.

"My God. Did she have an accident?" I asked Ronnie, the *Advance* photographer.

"Murdered," said Officer Tim Viera, another classmate from Lemoore High. "We've got a unit picking up Mike Warrington right now."

"Is he your primary suspect?"

"He's our only suspect. It's a known fact he was with her last night."

The Kings County forensic techs processed the crime scene and the media descended upon the town like a murder of crows. Lemoore was portrayed as a sleepy town untouched by homicide since 1996, and headlines blared INTERNATIONAL PHOTOGRAPHER SLAIN BY HOME TOWN LOVER. Evan kept some dignity in the *Advance* with discreet headlines and articles which spared the family.

A few days later I went to the county jail in Hanford to see if I could get ten minutes with Mike. Veronica Warrington was coming out of the visitors' section. Her homecoming-queen smile had turned to despair and matched her faded summer dress. "He didn't do it, Ginger," she said as she passed. But I needed to hear it from Mike.

He was a crumpled heap, a man who knew the world, and evidence, was against him.

"Mike, did you kill her?"

He looked dazed. "No."

"But you were there that night."

He cupped his hands over his face. "I went there to tell her I couldn't go through with it. She was mad and said a lot of hateful things, but I swear to God, she was alive when I walked out."

I believed him. Mike was long on charm and short on brains, but I'd never known him to be violent. Even on the football field he played the game with good sportsmanship. And although he was weak when it came to the need to be the focus of attention, he was a decent guy at heart.

But if Mike wasn't the killer, who hated Marta enough to murder her?

I went to the police station and found Tim.

"What's up, Ginger?"

"I wanted to offer my services in the Marta Ryan case."

"I'm all ears."

"I want to know if anyone processed the film in the Nikon that was in her bedroom."

He smiled a slow, laid-back grin. "You mean the camera trained on that spider? We haven't gotten around to that yet."

"Ronnie will let me process it over at the *Advance* darkroom."

"Marta was a bad influence on all of us. She's got you itching to do photography again." He grinned and thought it over. "Well, there could be a chain-of-evidence problem. But we don't expect anything important to be found on it—unless you think she was killed by a spider bite."

I took the 35-mm film over to the newspaper. Nobody was around, so I slipped into the darkroom. I found a voice-activated tape recorder on Bobby's desk and placed it on the processing table, well away from the trays of strong chemicals, so I could record any comments as I brought the images forth from the paper.

Marta had shown me the time lapse set up at about 2 P.M. Assuming the camera had been turned off at 6 A.M. when the body was found, there were seventeen frames exposed. I took each frame and slipped it into the enlarger and printed the frames on 8 x 10 paper. Like riding a bicycle, the developing process came back to me quickly. I tried several exposures and bathed the papers in vats of chemicals under the red lights, then removed them with tongs and laid them out to dry. When I was finished, I turned the lights on.

The black widow was shiny and fat. In some frames, the red hourglass was visible, gray in the black-and-white pictures. "The web would have stood out more if Marta had thought to put a black background behind the spider. But that would have made the spider hard to see," I said for the recorder.

It was on frame thirteen that I saw it. "There appears to be a shadow on the wall above the spider," I intoned.

"Is that right?" said Evan as he walked through the curtain of the darkroom

"I can't be sure," I said, squinting at the image. But I could be sure. It was a head with the outline of a fedora. Evan saw it, too.

"I had to do it, you know," Evan sighed. "She had no intention of taking him with her. She just wanted him to screw up his marriage and then she planned to leave him in the dust."

"How do you know?"

He gave a rueful smile. "She told me. She always told me what dirty tricks she was going to pull. She knew I'd love her no matter how cruel she was to other people. And that was the cruelest thing of all."

He picked up the photo and studied it before ripping it in

half. "I finally had to kill her. I killed the black widow, too. No reason for either of them to live and spread their poison. I really like you, Ginger, but Mike's got to take the rap for this. He wanted fame and fortune. He got infamy instead." Evan picked up the tray of acetic acid and came toward me. "I'm afraid you're going to have a little accident."

"Hold it right there." Tim slipped through the curtain and pointed his service revolver at Evan.

The acid flew across the room, soaking Tim's shirt. I picked up another tray of chemicals and dumped it on Evan's head, which produced howls of pain. Tim struggled to get the handcuffs on Evan.

I called the ambulance for both men. Tim had been protected by his bullet-proof vest and only suffered minor burns on his arms. Although the hat protected Evan from some of the chemicals, in the end, the fedora put him behind bars.

Even in death Marta wanted no part of us. Her body was shipped to Los Angeles where a massive funeral was attended by artists and fans. But we remembered her in Lemoore, all right. We just didn't miss her at the class reunion.

~

# Swan Song

J.A. LUCAS

Like a teenaged groupie following Fresno mayor Allen "Bubba" (*In The Heat Of The Night*) Autry, I returned to the scene of the crime early in the morning, yawning from the late hours I'd already put in there the night before. For the past two days the weather was having its way with us. The promiscuous tease had seduced the Central Valley into thoughts of a long, easy autumn, then followed with a contemptuous slap of bitter cold. I shivered; too bad it wasn't spring. I could see where this acre and a half of park would be a blooming eye-opener.

My boss, Chief Detective Inspector Thomas, already staked out the area. The man must never need sleep. Beside which, he'd been born a cross between a terrier and a bloodhound. Nothing escaped him, and working as his partner this past year beat all the courses I'd taken at the academy. Thing was, he didn't talk much except when flimflamming a suspect. On the job he grunted, twitched those graying eyebrows, or pulled on his earlobe and pursed his lips. Words, when they came, were pithy and direct.

Thomas was hunkered down on the muddy slope near the large pond to get a different perspective of the crime scene. In his warm brown jacket and slacks he looked like the Duncan Water Gardens' resident toad. I was hard put not to laugh.

Better cool it, Brian-my-boy, I told myself, it's way too early in the case to make with the wisecracks. I watched him closely. By interpreting the body language I could follow his thinking: Last night at early dusk the deceased, sixty-seven-year-old James Mercer, sat here on the bench where he could enjoy the shenanigans of water fowl and kaleidoscopic clusters of koi.

Not many people visit the gardens when it's cold, and James Mercer probably counted himself the park's only pleasure seeker. The caretaker stated that he always made rounds before he closed the gates at seven. He'd greeted Mercer yesterday around five-thirty, then went to his greenhouse to nurse the Australian ferns. Between five-thirty and seven when the caretaker discovered the body, James Mercer had met with one or more people. The damp ground showed prints where he stood up and turned to face his assailant. The assailant stayed on the gravel path, from where he stabbed a long, thin-bladed knife into Mercer's chest cavity. There was so much blood, the knife probably nicked his heart. Mercer didn't collapse on the spot, but staggered backwards, lost his footing, and slid down the muddy slope to the pond's edge. This scenario came from reading the evidence at the point of conflict.

Around the body area was a great deal of disturbance. The assailant or an accomplice had tried to reach the dead man from a nearby footbridge and either jumped or fell into the pond. We had some good casts of footprints and a couple of hand impressions where he leveraged himself out of the water. Hand and shoe size profiled probable male. The unknown subject lifted Mercer's wallet and left trails of muddy water on the front of the dead man's coat. But he didn't touch the Rolex watch or two valuable rings that were in plain sight. Too scared? Too stupid? Both?

Inspector Thomas inclined his head my way. "Garbage companies?"

"Called 'em first thing," I replied. "Only one of those places was due for pick up. Company agreed to delay until tomorrow."

He gave a quick nod.

"What do you think of the partner for doing Mercer?" I asked.

Thomas tugged his earlobe.

Translation: Didn't feel right.

I agreed; Mercer's business partner, Arthur Bowden, would benefit from full ownership of the RV franchise, but he was a sharp one. Wouldn't have left the jewelry if he were trying to make this look like a robbery gone wrong.

I told Thomas I checked on Bowden's movements; nothing conclusive. He might have been able to drive over from his office to do the deed, but he would have had to fly back to fit in the time window of the crime and his secretary's statement— unless she was in cahoots or bed with her boss.

The dead man's wife was out of it. Frail Rose Mercer had recently been moved by ambulance to a hospice to finish out her days.

The couple had no living children, only a niece by marriage on the wife's side. Said niece was the one Mercer planned on meeting today, and who had left a message on his answering machine last night saying she and her husband had arrived and were staying at Motel 6. A deputy was dispatched to escort them here this morning.

Meanwhile, I watched the comedy routine of a white swan near the crime scene. Charlie Tooms, evidence technician, finished taking pictures of the site by natural light and turned his camera toward the bird. The swan immediately stopped its wing-flapping, backpedaling antics on the water and slid into serene behavior. I heard Charlie mutter, "Damn ham," as he snapped off a couple of shots to placate the bird.

To keep warm Thomas and I tramped along the park's trails, scoping out the territory to get a fix on the probable route the murderer took. The feisty bird followed us via water, making several bids for attention. I called him Harpo, as I surmised the comedian was a Royal Mute swan. Must have felt a real kinship with my boss.

At ten o'clock Deputy Horner escorted a couple through the front gate. Thomas and I waited in a gazebo built out over the pond. I studied the newcomers as they approached. Both were in their late thirties or early forties. Woman tricked out in well-worn coat and shoes and carried an out-of-shape shoulder bag. Arms crossed close over her chest, no expression allowed on her face except for a tight mouth. Was she grieving or missing her morning coffee?

The man was built big and running to a paunch; orange gimme cap, flannel shirt, jeans. No coat and regretting it. Smiled a lot and looked clumsy.

A discreet cough and an eyebrow twitch from Thomas sent me back to check out the man's shoes. Damn, how'd I miss that one? They were white and shiny and new. Shirt and jeans appeared new, too. I called Thomas's brow and raised him a smirk.

Willy and Patty Stone were just up for a visit from Bakersfield. They arrived after eight last night and left the message for Patty's uncle. She insisted on doing all the talking now, while Willy stood behind her with a genial expression. I eyed the size of his hands and feet and checked off two more items that put him as a possible.

Harpo paced in the water.

When asked, Patty said they'd never been to the gardens before and had only been to Fresno once in the last seventeen years. Inspector Thomas became his most charming and took Patty Stone's arm to assist her up the path that led over the falls. Deputy Horner accompanied them.

I'd been given my instructions by brow signal and set about to become good ol' Willy Stone's new best friend. We walked along the pond's edge for a while before I let out a groan and motioned him to the nearest bench. Seated, I made a good show of a man with sore feet and slipped off my shoe.

"Oh, man," I said. "You know what they say about a cop's feet is true. What I wouldn't give to find a decent pair of shoes and not pay a month's salary for 'em." I turned to Willy. "Say, those look good, they comfortable?"

"Yeah, got to say they feel pretty good and din't cost no arm and leg." He stuck his feet out for me to admire his shoes.

"That so?" I asked. "But, I don't like spending a lot of time breaking in new shoes. How'd they feel the first day you wore 'em?"

"This *is* the first day, and they're just fine. Wife picked them up for me last night at that Target store just up the street from our motel. Only paid twenty-nine-ninety-five for 'em."

"Can't beat that."

I motioned to another deputy as we stood up, and the three of us made our way around the pond opposite Thomas and Mrs. Stone. Ol' Willy and I got along like a house a-fire, and Harpo looked disgusted. Willy told me how he liked to tinker with motors and engines. Picked them up at swap meets, hokeyed them around until they ran again, and then sold them at the next meet.

"Well, hey!" I said. "You'll want to see how they got this baby to pump those falls. Come on over here."

I led the three of us along the path and over one of the footbridges. I stopped them at the bridge's end, bent down, and pointed for Willy to look at the area underneath. Willy started to squat to see, but jumped up immediately when he realized Harpo was making a dead set at him.

"Oh no, you don't, bird! You're not getting me again." He turned to me. "You know what that damned duck did to me yesterday? He *goosed* me, that's what he did. Never saw the like. You'd better be careful of where you set."

I stood up, "Yesterday huh? That's mighty interesting. Did you fall into the water, maybe got all muddy, too, and had to buy new clothes last night?"

"That's right. Couldn't get no jacket, though. But, I tell you that's the darnedest bird—"

"Willy!"

Patty Stone hurried down the terraced steps and joined us. Thomas and Deputy Horner followed.

"Hi, Patty, I was just telling—"

"*Willy*, I told you *I'd* do the talking." Patty gave his arm a jerk. She turned to us. "Willy sometimes gets things confused."

"But, Patty, din't you see what that loco bird done? It was just like last night. You said yourself it weren't my fault. That bird has it in for me, I swear!"

A woman scorned has nothing on a scornful woman. Patty Stone called her husband several names all meaning "fool" and shoved him backwards into the water. Harpo swam circles around his prey and hissed.

We got Patty restrained and Willy out of the water and into some blankets. Charlie, the technician, signaled he'd gotten it all on film. With the testimony of the two deputies and evidence of the shoes and clothes we were sure to find, either in their car, room, or motel's garbage Dumpster, we pretty much had a lock on this case. Maybe we'd find the knife there, too.

While we waited for the warrants to be faxed to the patrol car, I looked fondly at the beautiful bird. If he'd been a dog, I'd have given him a bone. As it was, Harpo swanned his arrogance of the couple before an appreciative audience.

"Bravo, Harpo," I told him.

He acknowledged this as his due and glided off with a last twitch of his tail feathers.

Shivering and beat, Willy got tired of his wife calling him a fool and told us how Patty Stone had talked with her uncle earlier yesterday. Mercer told her of his plans to be here and said he would meet with them later at his house. Patty wasn't doing later and killed Mercer here with a kitchen knife she'd brought from home. She made Willy go after the wallet, and that's when he got his mud bath.

Patty figured that if Mercer died before his wife, she would inherit all from her aunt. But like a lot of greedy bullies, Patty Stone lacked the nerve to do the deed all by herself. So, she was done in by a smart bird and her own bird-brained husband.

Inspector Thomas and I made a farewell tour of the gardens. Back at the gazebo we watched Harpo frolic with a black swan.

"You know," I said, "I'm thinking of calling him Nemesis and writing a story about this case. What do you think of 'Nibbled by Nemesis' as a title?"

Thomas pursed his lips and whistled silently. I waited him out. He rocked back on his heels with his hands in his pockets and smiled. "'Two Stones With One Bird'."

~

# Tunnel Vision

SUNNY FRAZIER

Jeremy Hodges took one last look around to make sure the place was spotless. It wasn't easy to make dirt look tidy, and Jeremy was proud of his efforts. The Forestiere Underground Gardens had never looked as presentable as it did at this moment.

Today was the day the man from Los Angeles would be visiting.

"First impressions are always important," Jeremy said aloud. He often talked to himself these days since visitors had dwindled to a trickle. Not like the old days when the Underground Gardens was the number one tourist attraction in Fresno.

He was just out of high school when he landed the summer job as tour guide fifteen years ago. The subterranean chambers were dark and cool while the rest of Fresno roasted topside. The shyness that had plagued him all his life disappeared. He enjoyed the sound of his voice echoing off the earthen walls. When people listened intently as he lectured on the history of the gardens and Baldasare Forestiere's dream, it made Jeremy feel important. He knew he would never leave.

Jeremy felt a spiritual kinship with the Italian immigrant. Baldasare came to Fresno hoping to plant orange trees and lemon trees, but ended up with ten acres of hardpan. Instead of giving up, Baldasare went down. What started out as a cellar to es-

104

cape the summer heat turned into forty years of carving and sculpting the earth. Baldasare created an underground retreat unlike anything seen before. People called him crazy, but California Historical Landmark #916 billed the Italian as "unbounded by conventionality."

Baldasare's story kept Jeremy going when topsiders referred to him as "The Mole." Even the owners scoffed at his subterranean obsession. "You're looking a little pale, Jeremy," they would jibe. "You need to get more sun," they'd say as they counted the day's revenues.

Not that there was much in the coffers to count. Things had gone downhill over the years. But the visitor from Los Angeles was about to change all that.

Footsteps echoed down the walkway leading into the reception area. No tour groups were expected today. Jeremy straightened his tie, smoothed his collar, and stood at attention behind the reception desk.

The man from L.A. wore sunglasses and a Dodger baseball cap. He had three-day stubble and sported a Nike polo shirt that matched his hightops. Baggy shorts showed off knobby knees.

"This place smells like dirt!" the visitor announced as he pulled off his sunglasses and squinted at the earthen walls in bewilderment.

"It's the famous Underground Gardens," explained Jeremy. "You're underground."

"Right, right. I shoulda figured that one out. Are you the kid that's gonna give me the ten-cent tour?"

Jeremy introduced himself and extended his hand. The man stared at it for a second, then gave it one quick pump and released his hold.

"Forestiere was an Italian immigrant who came to Fresno in 1906 and began to sculpt the garden," Jeremy began.

"Hey kid," interrupted the man from L.A. "I'm not buying a

history lesson. Just walk me through this place so I don't get lost. I wouldn't want to stay in these tunnels forever."

Perhaps the man had already read the brochures before making the trip north, Jeremy reasoned. He was disappointed that he couldn't give the spiel he'd practiced for three days. But the beauty and awe of the Underground Gardens would speak for itself.

"This way," said Jeremy. He led the man to the Great Hall.

The vast room always inspired visitors. Small windows just above ground level filtered fingers of light into the room. At one time dances were held here as the elite of Fresno society two-stepped to Big Band tunes. Now it seemed like a cavern within a cavern.

The Great Hall had no effect on this visitor. Neither did the grottoes, the bedrooms, the kitchen or the library. He ignored the orange trees growing up through the round holes cut into the ceiling and seemed oblivious to the beautiful rock archways.

"It smells bad in here, kinda like a mildew stink," he commented. "Gotta do something about that or people won't come."

"Visitors expect an earthy odor," Jeremy said testily. "It's the famous Underground Gardens."

"Not for long, son. I plan to turn this loser into an amusement park."

The visitor walked ahead, leaving Jeremy behind in stunned silence. An amusement park? "You must be mistaken," he said, rushing to catch up with the visitor. "This is a state treasure. Next to Yosemite, it's the top landmark in the area!"

"I tried to get Yosemite, but they weren't selling," growled the man. "And there ain't nothin' special about this place, kid. Some crazy man dug a tunnel and lived in it. It's a hole, not a landmark."

The visitor ignored Jeremy's hand-lettered no admittance sign and entered a small room which had suffered El Niño damage. A deep trench scarred the floor. Later that day Jeremy planned to pour cement to reinforce support beams to keep the walls from crumbling.

"I'm gonna turn this ten-acre eyesore into The Underground-a-Rama, the world's first subterranean theme park." The man's eyes glittered as he described his vision: a roller coaster that would dive beneath the surface of the earth. Dante's Merry-Go-Round in the Great Hall. A haunted cavern. "And I'm going to tear out all these stupid fruit trees. Whoever heard of growing trees under the ground?"

It was too much to bear. Jeremy grabbed a handy two-by-four and swung at the back of the stranger's head. The man fell into the trench, his neck twisted at a very odd angle.

It took two weeks for the police to drop by. They'd traced the L.A. entrepreneur to Underground Gardens. Jeremy told them that the man missed his appointment and offered to give the officers a free tour. The policemen politely declined.

Too bad. They were the first visitors to drop by since Jeremy had completed the new addition and he was dying to show it off. The garden of white lilies covering the unsightly trench was his best inspiration to date. The blooms thrived on the filtered light, humidity, and a very special fertilizer. Jeremy even hand-lettered a sign reading BLEST IN PEACE.

Baldasare would be so proud.

~

# ~CULTURE & CONSEQUENCES~

# Nighthawks

CORA J. RAMOS

C Street in Fresno was not a street to linger on. The air currents swirling in a chaotic dance unsettled the homeless drunks moving in the shadows. Red neon lights from a bar reflected off the wet pavement like dabs of vermillion from the tip of an Impressionist's paintbrush. Splashed blood. Clarissa tried not to think of Salvador's death in artistic terms, but couldn't help herself.

A man stepped forward carrying a sign marked JUDGEMENT. "Those who transgress are doomed." He glared at her.

She hurried through the intermittent swaths of light around the lampposts, avoiding him. She felt responsible enough for Salvador's death; she didn't need some doomsday prophet telling her she was going to hell. But she couldn't walk around aimlessly all night ruminating over it, either.

She kicked a bottle cap, sending it tumbling down the street like a noisy castanet. It landed in front of Phillies'. A good place to stop.

Yellowing lamps infused the diner with a sullenness thick as an impasto painting. A couple talked low at the far end of the counter and a lone man sat staring into his cup.

After finding a seat at the other end, Clarissa noticed the print of Edward Hopper's *Nighthawks* hung high on the wall next to the clock. Beneath it was a copy painted in oil. As she looked at it more closely, she saw that the three people sitting along the counter wore present-day clothing like those in the painting of Phillies'. Instead of a waiter in a white cap, the painting depicted a redheaded waitress like the real one leaning against the counter by the coffeepots, staring at her nails. She looked up when Clarissa noticed her.

"Something to eat, honey? " She walked over and slid a menu in front of Clarissa.

Clarissa pushed it back.

"Just coffee."

She fixated on a crumb in front of her and mulled over whether or not to wipe it away. She tried hard to push down the guilt that saturated every fiber. Had she really been responsible?

From a dark recess in her mind, she saw Salvador's face smiling like he had that first time they'd met. His charm and good looks had made her feel desirable, worthy. Even though her gut had warned her he was trouble, she'd let him into her life.

The control started first in small ways—flattery that made her want to please him, subtle expectations that prompted guilt-laden explanations for why she was the slightest bit late or hadn't worn his favorite dress or fixed his favorite food. Gentle coaxing that she meet his needs. His subtlety soon dissolved into more insistent demands. She'd tried to get some space from him, but he wouldn't have it. Phone calls from him had plagued her at the studio. Then the voiceless, menacing silences before the hang-up clicks. She began to feel uncomfortable.

That night when she'd been out with her girlfriends and caught a glimpse of him watching her from behind a pillar, it came together. She realized the gravity of her situation. He was the one who'd killed her cat when she had refused to see him again. He was the one who'd sent the threatening notes—words cut from newspapers, untraceable warnings of her impending death. She'd awakened from her cloud-covered reverie and saw the nightmare reality. Salvador, who seemed to have everything—good looks, money, and a prestigious job—was a stalker. There was no telling how far he'd go.

So, had she knowingly goaded him to come after her across the boulevard tonight? It all happened so fast. She'd been staring defiantly at him when he appeared to motion her over. Had she seen the light turn red and known that in his rage at her refusal to come, he'd chase after her and be struck by that speeding car?

She couldn't erase the image of the red liquid seeping out from beneath his broken skull and the crude reflection of the neon lights in his blood. She couldn't stop feeling guilty.

### Marlita

Marlita put the scratched, worn mug of coffee down with a loud thud. *Something bad bothering that one.* She asked if the girl wanted cream. The girl didn't look up, just shook her head.

"Well, I'll leave your bill open, just in case you change your mind. We have some pretty good lemon meringue pie. Fresh today."

The girl just stared at a crumb on the counter and shook her head slowly. Marlita felt the hair on her neck rise and sensed the girl's guilt. It was without justification, she was sure of that.

### Forkner

The damp cold of the night seeped into Forkner's bones. He parked next to the dark alley under the lamppost, keys plainly visible. He was halfway down the street from what looked like a diner named Phillies'. He looked at his watch. It was eleven twenty-five, twenty minutes since hitting that man. Driving away had been a mistake, but he'd panicked. He'd be ruined if they'd caught him DUI one more time, probably jail time to boot. The thought of throwing his legal career down the toilet was more than he could bear even if it meant the death of that guy he hit.

He couldn't even remember how he'd gotten here to C Street. He'd driven around aimlessly, trying to devise a plan and gambling no one had seen him hit the guy in the dark. Nobody around here would notice the broken headlight, but without a doubt somebody would make short work of stealing his car in this neighborhood. As soon as someone ripped it off, he would report it stolen—hours earlier. He wanted a double shot of whiskey badly, something to drive out the demons. But more importantly, he needed the alibi that Phillies' diner would afford, and he needed to sober up before calling the police.

He pushed open the heavy swinging door, past the man who was leaving. The wind gusted in with him, stirring the quiet gloom. The couple near the door turned to face the disturbance, then wilted back into hushed conversation. He took a seat at the counter where he could watch his car. He was sure nobody here would remember what time he'd come in. He had to remember to get a receipt.

The waitress put a steaming mug of coffee in front of him and slapped down a greasy menu before he could open his mouth. She was off to the corner to refill the cup of the pretty woman sitting alone.

*Jake*

Jake stopped when he reached the alley and shifted the instrument case under his other arm. Under the streetlight, he leaned against the warm hood of the Mercedes with the busted headlight and felt around in his shirt pocket. He pulled out the joint and lit it. His previous high was wearing off and he needed to re-shape reality again. He'd shoved Salvador into the street tonight but the car hit him. Not his fault. It was a bad scene. What was he going to do? Hope nobody saw him.

Music came from an open window off the alley; static-filled jazz from a radio tuned to an AM station. He tapped his foot for a few moments to the old Charlie Parker rendition of "Blues for Alice" while he took a couple of drags.

He pushed the cigarette out against the lamppost, squeezed off the ash, and stuffed it back into his shirt pocket for later. Shifting the case back under his right arm, he turned up his collar and headed across the street to Phillies'.

He opened the door and stepped aside for the couple leaving. Marlita was removing their dirty dishes from the counter and slipping the tip into her pocket. She nodded at him and turned toward the coffeepot. He sat two seats away from a man in an Armani suit. *Out of place here. That Mercedes down the street must be his.*

Marlita wiped the counter and put a mug down in front of him. He nodded toward the pretty girl. "She from around here?"

"Not your type, Jake." Marlita poured the coffee without saying another word.

*I'll be famous one of these days. Then I'll have all the women I want, and everyone will know I'm somebody. Won't have to put up with no more snotty waitresses.* He pushed away the possibility that he might become famous for the wrong reason. He didn't want to think about that, but the events of earlier in the evening wouldn't leave him.

Salvador had been bugging him for some smack. He told him no. Didn't want anything to do with that dude. But then Salvador had grabbed his arm. He'd pushed him away. Wasn't his fault Salvador fell into the street. It happened so fast. Well, if the police came for him at the Blue Note at least he'd make the headlines. His fifteen minutes of fame. *Musician plays the blues after pushing man to his death.* Any publicity was good publicity, wasn't that the saying?

He should have called the police right away, told them it was an accident, but then they might have noticed he was high and probed enough to find out he was dealing a little heroin on the side. They wouldn't understand it was just to make ends meet. Could have gotten messy. Better he lay low and hope for the best.

The guy that hit Salvador probably called 911 to get an ambulance, anyway, so why was he worried?

Marlita slid a menu in front of him. "Gonna eat tonight?" She barely waited for him to shake his head before grabbing it back and heading toward the guy in the fancy suit.

*Marlita*

"What'll ya have?" She noticed the dark Mercedes across the street.

"A toasted bagel for now."

"Hey, this ain't uptown. We have donuts." She nodded toward the pie shelf. "Or a slice of lemon meringue."

"Just bring me some wheat toast."

When she shrugged and turned, she got one of those pictures in her mind—a dark car hit a man and knocked him down. She looked back at the man in the fancy suit. He was the one in the dark blue car, the dark Mercedes down the street.

If only she could stop them, the psychic flashes, end their growing intrusion. At first she'd joked with Doris about the funny stuff she was picking up from customers. Now it was more frequent, more serious—not so much fun learning about other people's dark secrets. She had begun to suspect she was somehow able to change things, mete out a sort of justice. But she had those time lapses and she wasn't sure.

Jake held up his cup for more coffee and she went to refill it, watching the man in the suit out of the corner of her eye. "You gonna play tonight? I see you got your sax."

"Yeah, over in the Tower District."

*A flash, again—another picture:* Jake arguing with a man on the street. The man grabbed Jake's arm and spun him around. Jake twisted his arm free with such force that the man was caught off guard and turned to keep himself from falling. Just as he turned, the falling man's eyes met the eyes of the woman across the street. At the same time he reached out to gain his balance, the heel of his boot slid off the curb and he had no time to react before falling in front of the speeding Mercedes. Jake walked away. Bad mistake.

But she'd clearly seen the man that fell, the bastard who got her daughter pregnant—that no-good bum Salvador. He turned his back on her little Shirley. Broke her heart and ruined her life. So, Salvador ate it tonight and guilt was on the menu. This time it was personal. She wiped away a tear and looked up at the clock. It was 11:45. She hurried back to the girl who didn't belong here.

"Look, honey, you gotta go. The coffee is free. Just head out the door and forget whatever happened earlier tonight. The guilt's not worth it."

"No, I need to sit here for a while, I can't go yet."

"Listen, I'm gonna tell you something and I want you to listen and take it to heart. My daughter, Shirley, she was a good girl, a little shy maybe but very gullible. I tried my best to toughen her up, make her smart to the ways of the world, the rotten guys to stay away from. But she went and fell for a guy that flattered and used her. She got pregnant and he hightailed it away, nowhere to be found. I didn't say nothin' to comfort her, just let her stew about it to make her realize she blew it. My little Shirley committed suicide. I'll never stop feeling guilty about that. Some guys are not worth worrying about. You know what I mean?"

Marlita looked over at Jake, knowing he was guilty of dealing crack and ruining people's lives, skimming on the edge. But now it was about murder and this time he'd pay. When she glanced at the man in the fancy suit, she knew he was selfish and greedy and wouldn't worry if someone died so long as he got what he wanted. He'd pay tonight, also.

Clarissa reached out and touched her hand. "I know you're just trying to help, and you're right about my problem being a guy, but I'm not pregnant. It's more serious than that, not to make light of what happened to your daughter."

Marlita looked at the clock. It was 11:50. "Honey, I don't have time to explain it right now. I'm not even sure I understand it, so I'm going to say this blunt-like. Salvador was a bum. Whatever happened, he had it coming. Don't go feeling in any way guilty. You had nothing to do with it. I know this. The others in here, they'll have to pay the piper—locked forever in the consequences of their actions."

She looked up at the painting on the wall. Clarissa followed her gaze.

"Don't ask me any questions but get out of here, right now, okay?"

*Clarissa*

How did the waitress know about Salvador? Clarissa got chills as she looked up at the painting. The people in the painting had changed. They looked like the two men sitting in the diner—and her. How could that be?

She felt the instinct to run. She'd failed to run when she had this feeling before, when she first met Salvador. It cost her dearly. She had promised herself never to fail to follow her intuition again.

She got up, left a tip on the counter and hurried out the door. The man with the JUDGEMENT sign glared at her as he walked past. She shivered, and glanced back into Phillies'. The lights had been lowered and a waiter with a white cap was locking the door. The diner was empty. How could that be?

She stepped back to look in at the painting of *Nighthawks*. The figures of the well-dressed man and the musician with the sax were the ones sitting in the painting now—and the waitress looking out of the window, smiling.

~

# Sayonara, Mr. Chips

SUNNY FRAZIER

I was the only Japanese P.I. in Fresno—that's why the Yanakoras called me at 6 A.M. before dialing 911. Toru Yanakora, CEO of Yankee Systems, leading producer of mini-micro computer chips, was dead. Murdered, to be precise.

I entered the home study, rich with silk wall hangings, a fine porcelain tea set, and the body of Yanakora. Red blood stood out on the breast of his white suit.

"Mr. Oshikane." A tiny sparrow of a woman with fine rice powder softening her wrinkles took dainty steps toward me. Her rose kimono floated like a lily upon a pad. "I am so glad you could come quickly. Please inspect the room and my husband. When you are done, I will call the police."

I bowed as low as my four-hundred-fifty pounds would allow me and went to work. I presumed the wife had already removed any dirty pictures or tokens that might make the great man lose face. It is honorable that a man should have such things, but dishonorable to be caught dead with them.

Casing the room, I noted in my steno pad that one cup was missing from a four-cup sake set, and one cup had a chip. Yanakora was a man of great wealth—he could well afford to replace the set. Carefully arranged flowers rested in an alcove.

I finished my cursory examination before the police arrived. I tried to make myself invisible as they rushed in, wrapped the

119

room in yellow crime-scene tape, photographed the body, and interviewed the bodyguards. Mrs. Yanakora told the guards they should commit hara-kiri for allowing her husband to die. Since we were in America, I suggested she fire them instead.

A homicide detective approached me.

"Name and address?" he began without preliminaries.

I gave him the information in broken English. However, when he asked why I was at the home, I looked to the family. It would look suspicious that a private detective was called before the authorities. Too many questions. A small lie was better.

"I am sumo wrestler. Yanakora-san support my career."

A little lie in broken English, not too far from the truth. The detective looked me up and down, a rude practice I have grown used to. He snorted like a horse.

"You're a big one, all right. Well, your benefactor's gone to the big pagoda in the sky. Guess you'll have to find someone else to keep your rice bowl filled. We're through with you here."

The insult about food made me hungry rather than mad. I climbed into my modified Volvo with all seats removed, replaced by a single reinforced seat, and picked up three foot-long tuna sandwiches on the way back to my office. It was on the ground floor of a very old building because I find elevators and stairs difficult. The office was large enough for living quarters in the rear. I kept a futon, a refrigerator, and an alley cat named Fuji who shared my taste for seafood.

As I set out two plates, I pondered my words to the policeman. There is some truth in every lie, just as there is a lie within all truths.

I was called Daikon, "Radish," when I first became a sumo *rikishi* because I was hot-headed, and because of what the silk *mawashi* hid in its soft diaper folds. I let the boys tease me as I ate and fleshed out, dreaming of one day being *Yokozuna*, Grand Sumo Champion.

That dream changed the day my hero, Noruma, won the title of Grand Champion. We celebrated with platters of white tuna and sushi. Sake flowed like a crystal river. During the reverie, Noruma disappeared. I found him in a deserted hallway, tears falling on the silk of his kimono.

"Why do you cry at the time of your greatest glory?" I asked.

"Because I have achieved my best. Now I must fight to keep my title or walk away from the ring forever." Noruma hung his head.

"You will win many more fights," I insisted.

"The fight I lose is the one people will remember. I shall quit with honor."

And that's what the great man did. His topknot was cut from his head and ceremonially presented to him as fans wept. And I left the ring forever because I would not want to be the one to bring a giant like Noruma down.

I chose to be a private eye because my powers of observation were keen and my mind could see how life and death were often intertwined. I moved to America where people are more suspicious and therefore in need of private eyes. And I found that a fat man is often underestimated and not considered a threat.

"Fuji," I said dividing the first sandwich with the cat, "a prominent man died today. Who would help such a great man pass from this life?" I often consulted the cat on important cases, but this time she was busy eating.

Who ate from the plate of Mr. Yanakora? I put down my second sandwich and wiped my fingers before picking up the steno pad. The police would suspect the family. I did not suspect them. I saw their silent, profound grief as they held their heads high and rigid in respect. The police would call them cold and unfeeling.

Who else was at Yanakora's table? The workers of the plant who depended on their boss's success for their daily bread. I decided to go to the plant and take a look around while the investigation team was occupied at the house.

I offered the rest of the sandwich to Fuji, who had been eyeing it and now graciously accepted. The third tuna sandwich was for the road. I wrapped it up and slipped it into my coat pocket.

The Yankee Systems plant was in its own little industrial park on the outskirts of the city. It was surrounded by shrubbery that must have been trimmed with tweezers. A waterfall fell from the second floor terrace into a koi pond that circled the building like a moat. A raised Japanese bridge crossed the pond to the entrance. Workers tossed food to the fish.

I expected to be greeted by a samurai, but a pretty Western woman acknowledged me from behind the counter. I bowed and expressed condolences on the death of her boss. By the look on her face, now whiter than rice powder, I knew she had not been informed. She picked up the phone and called for someone.

Mac Taylor did not return my bow. His words were abrupt. "We should talk in private."

He led me down a maze of hallways until we reached a paneled office of fine teak.

"You say Mr. Yanakora is dead?"

"Murdered, to be precise."

He looked at me, disbelieving. His hand reached for the phone.

"The grieving widow is with the police now. I'm sure they will question you very soon. That is why we must hurry. Are all important papers in this desk?"

"Whoa." Taylor tried to block me, a gnat in front of a boulder. "Where do you fit into this picture?"

"The family has asked me to investigate, in addition to the officials." I shouldered him aside and went to the desk. "Police eyes see only the crime. My eyes slant to see the suggestion of a crime."

I let him chew on that while I went through neat stacks of mail. "Did Mr. Yanakora receive any threatening letters?"

Taylor shrugged. "If he did, he wouldn't tell me. He had enemies, of course. Anyone in his position would have to watch his back."

A day planner was on the desk. I asked Taylor to pick it up to avoid leaving my fingerprints. I had him flip the pages backwards. Most of the entries were in English. I paid attention to the ones in Japanese script. Several times I jotted the lines on the notepad.

A yellow sticky note next to the computer caught my eye. Two names of streets, Fulton and Divisadero, written in Japanese. I slipped it in my pocket and felt it stick on the wrapped tuna sandwich.

"May I please see the workers?"

Taylor looked uncomfortable. "The observation gallery is upstairs. I'm not sure your," he hesitated, "stamina would hold out."

He was afraid I would break the slender staircase. "I see cameras mounted on the walls. Perhaps there is a camera in the work area?"

Like a thief caught with jade in his hands, Taylor nodded. "We trust the employees, but..."

He took me to a door marked UTILITY CLOSET and opened it. A bank of monitors glowed on the wall. Taylor asked the security guard to leave—to give me room, not privacy.

I watched as the camera scanned the soul of Yankee Systems. Hundreds of workers, each at a station, staring into microscopes and nimbly working on the mini-micro chips. They wore white jackets like doctors. The room was painted bright white and the floor was white linoleum. Soft classical music flowed through the sterile room.

"Do the workers enjoy their work?"

"They get paid well," was Taylor's reply.

"One does not equate with the other."

Taylor turned to me. "If you're asking if anyone down there had a motive to kill Yanakora, the answer is no. How many bosses know every worker by name? How many send gifts to their families? He put on ice cream socials and kite-flying events during business hours. And to top it off, every employee got stock in the company."

Happy children, I thought. What would happen to the company now?

Appearing on the screen was a heavily tattooed man pushing a cart. He did not have on a technician's coat. The black lines on his arms and neck looked like dirty linen among white sheets.

"This man," I smudged the screen with my finger, "he does not belong."

"Yes, he's one of Mr. Yanakora's charity cases. He started working here two months ago." Taylor put his nose up in the air and sniffed. "Do you smell something fishy?"

"Tuna." And tattoos. I knew what I must look for at Fulton and Divisadero. Bowing, I left the building just as the police were pulling up.

Fulton is a street lined with fine buildings gone to seed. Divisadero is an inauspicious beginning of downtown Fresno. Where they meet, the lines blur. Buildings fall in despair to the decay that undermines their foundations. People also fall.

This is where the Yakuza thrive.

I parked the Volvo carefully, knowing its presence and mine would be signaled around the neighborhood before I took ten steps. Sure enough, figures appeared from the shadows.

"I am looking for the man who will tell me truths among lies," I called out in Japanese.

Laughter. "Go back to Tokyo, fat boy."

"I'm looking for the man with tattoos in his eyes."

This time there was no laughter. The silence lengthened with the shadows of late afternoon.

"He wants to know what business you have with him."

A gang member, bald and tattooed all over his head, stepped out of the shadows.

I was not intimidated. Being larger than most human beings, I'm usually able to hold my own. If not, a .45 in my pocket evens the odds. Unfortunately, all I was armed with today was a tuna sandwich.

"I am not police, I work privately. I need information. Tell him it is Daikon."

More laughter from the shadows. Then I was motioned forward.

The apartment was dank and smelled worse than my pocket of tuna. I made my way to the center of an empty room where a man sat on the only chair. I knew him as Hirsu. Legend had it that he had the inside of his eyelids tattooed so only he could see the secret symbols.

"You are a long way from the *dohyo*, Daikon. You wear a suit now." He laughed, teeth and missing teeth shone like a piano keyboard.

I bowed. "A long way, Hirsu. Western clothes do not suit me. I will be in my kimono at the end of our conversation."

"Ahh, kimono. It's been a long time since I felt the folds around me."

"Allow me to buy you a kimono, Hirsu-san."

He cocked his head and scowled. "A cotton one?"

"I would not dishonor you. It would be silk." And it would cost me my retainer. "A few questions only, and seconds of your time in return."

Hirsu dismissed the gang members, who left mumbling insults and threats. "Children pretending to be thugs. Now, get to your business."

"A man has been killed today. An important man."

"Yanakora."

It did not surprise me that he knew. The Japanese community is very small.

"We didn't kill him."

"No, Hirsu. But I found a note in his office." I reached in and pulled the sticky note off the sandwich. It was oil-stained.

He sniffed the note. "So?"

"Even the wealthy Yanakora knows that Hirsu knows more. And Hirsu knows that the only way his son can get out of the Yakuza life is to work for such a man. Heh?"

Hirsu chuckled. "It was worth a try. The boy will screw up, you'll see."

"Why did Yanakora contact you?"

"He wanted a special favor. So special he would dirty his shoes to visit me. So special he kneeled in the filth of these mats and bowed before me like a servant." Hirsu leaned forward. "He wanted to know how to bring over one of the hidden ones from the old country."

Startled, I asked, "What did you tell him?"

"I said 'Why go across the ocean when you can find one on your own beach?' " He leaned back and howled with laughter.

"Hirsu, can you contact this man and ask him to visit me?" I pulled out a business card, which I made myself on the computer, Japanese on one side, English on the other.

"What will you give me now if I say yes?"

I pulled out the tuna sandwich, hoping it would not give him ptomaine poisoning. I was sure he'd eaten worse in a lifetime.

The trade was acceptable. I made my way out of the cellar, Hirsu's blessing as my protection. I climbed into the Volvo, which still had four tires and four hubcaps, and left the area. I might have breathed a sigh of relief but I knew that by giving my business card to Hirsu I had walked into the dragon's mouth.

~

Two days passed. I talked to Mrs. Yanakora, who politely inquired as to whether my investigation had revealed anything. The police, she explained, were interviewing all of the workers at the plant and disrupting business. She did not believe they would find the murderer. I assured her I had a few leads.

The *Fresno Bee* and the *Wall Street Journal* hinted that Yanakora had stolen the mini-micro chip design and this was retaliation. CNN suggested the son was behind the patricide in the ultimate hostile takeover. "A chip off the old block," David Letterman joked. I waited for the dragon to make his appearance.

It was the knife at the throat that I first noticed. Not the jimmied door, not the silent footsteps across the mats. Even Fuji did not flick a whisker.

My business card was flung down on my chest.

"Thank you for coming," I said in shaky Japanese. "Would you care for tea?"

He kept the knife at my throat. "Do you have soda?"

He let me rise off the futon and go to the refrigerator. Only two sodas left—I hoped he liked Dr Pepper. A preference for Coke could cost me my life.

My visitor slipped up the scarf covering his face just enough to sip the drink. His eyes watched me without blinking.

"I would like to talk to you about Mr. Yanakora's death." I picked my words carefully like stones arranged in a pond.

He nodded and waited.

"He contacted Hirsu two months ago and asked to be put in touch with you."

The cold eyes bored into me.

"There is only one reason to hire an assassin. Who did Mr. Yanakora want killed?"

"A man very close to him." The voice was low and guttural. "His son?"

The assassin waited.

"Mac Taylor?"

Nothing.

"Did you kill your target?"

"I completed the request, yes."

"And do you know who killed Mr. Yanakora?"

"Yes."

He turned away from me then and stared at Fuji.

I tried to get back on his good side. "I've heard that a ninja can tell the time by looking in a cat's eye. Is that true?"

He turned back and gave me a withering glare.

"What time is it from her eyes?"

"Time for me to leave," he rasped. He turned to slip away like a ghost.

"Please, give me something," I begged.

He reached into a pouch hanging from a belt and placed a sharp object in my hand. "A secret is safe with two men only if one is dead."

With that, he melted into the night.

I read my notes the next morning over a dozen scrambled eggs, half a loaf of bread, and two cartons of orange juice. Everything fell into harmony, like a haiku poem. I called Mrs. Yanakora to inquire if this was a good time to drop by. Then I climbed in the car and drove to the house.

Mrs. Yanakora was alone. She offered green tea and sea-weed crackers, which I politely refused until she insisted.

I brushed the crumbs off my suit and said, "Mrs. Yanakora, I have discovered who killed your husband. Please come with me to his study."

At the door of the study I stopped. "Look at the room. The mats have been changed. Things have been removed. Do you remember how it was when you discovered him four days ago?"

I consulted my notes. "Your husband was here." I pointed to

the floor. "His back was to the window. He was kneeling on a pillow and reading."

She was nodding as I continued. "There is one cup missing from the sake set, and one cup with a chip." I reached into my pocket and pulled out the sharp object that the ninja had given me. It slipped into the chipped area and no crack was visible. "The killer made your husband drop the sake cup. He kept the chip as proof of his crime. The other sake cup is missing in respect to show that your husband is gone from this world.

"Do you remember the flowers in the room that morning? A simple arrangement of one white chrysanthemum with three white roses. Beautiful, but more appropriate for a funeral."

"He loved to arrange flowers," she said, and dabbed her eyes. Rice powder rubbed off showing sallow skin underneath.

"Finally, he was wearing a white suit. He dressed for death and waited. But death told time by the cat's eye and came when it was ready."

"I must be a stupid woman, Detective Oshikane. I don't understand what you're talking about."

I wrapped my large hands around her small ones. "Mrs. Yanakora, your husband had a doctor's appointment two months ago. It was on his appointment calendar at work. I looked up the doctor's name and found him under 'Oncologists.' Your husband had cancer."

Her mouth opened, forming a little "O."

"He will not show a detective his medical records, but I'm sure he would show you."

"He was going to die anyway," she said faintly.

"So he hired an assassin to kill him."

Mrs. Yanakora looked into my eyes. "My husband committed suicide with the hand of another."

"Yes," I agreed. I bowed to show my respect.

I bowed even lower when I saw my check.

~

Fuji rewarded me for a case well done by sniffing my pocket and purring. I was obligated to return the gesture with fish treats, which have no fish in them at all. She doesn't care.

As I stroked her, I thought that the Sumo Way was not so different from life in general. Sumo Master Noruma worked his way up to *Yokozuna* and found his only choice was to lose or leave. Mr. Yanakora was the *Yokozuna* of the microchip world, the Grand Master. Having reached the top of his game, there were suddenly no more choices for him. He could slowly lose his ability to run his company because of cancer—or he could leave. Both men chose to leave while still on the peak of the mountain.

The Yanakoras steered clients my way, and I renamed my business "Daikon Detective Agency." Hirsu received a silk kimono, which he was buried in soon after. The police still have the case open and chase their tails.

I have never seen the assassin again.

That is a good thing.

~

# Myth, Magic, and Madness

CORA J. RAMOS

*It'd been worth it. The months of traveling down the Amazon, trekking into the interior, enduring the bugs, animals, and snakes, in order to bring these treasures out of the jungle had all been worth it.*

Kama put the finishing touches on the Myth and Magic exhibit at the Fresno Art Museum, flicked on the lighting, and stood back to admire her handiwork. Shadows around the masks, weapons, and musical instruments created exactly the aura of mystery she wanted. The intricate designs on the hand-carved hardwood bowls stood out dramatically against the stark simplicity of the statues.

Linda ducked her head in the doorway. "Hey, it looks great, but you better get some rest for the opening tomorrow. That stomachache you had earlier is not a good sign. Judy and I are leaving now."

"I'm fine. I'll come and lock up behind you. I have a few more things to finish."

"You don't look very good, Kama."

"Don't worry about me. When this exhibit opens tomorrow, I'll finally get the national recognition I've been working so hard for—maybe I'll be offered that position at the Met in New York. Then I'll feel great and it will all have been worth it."

Linda frowned and looked at her oddly. "How can you say that? What about Sean?"

"He'd agree."

Linda looked horrified. "Kama! You can't mean that."

Kama held the door open as Linda and Judy stepped outside, wondering what Linda was so upset about. Linda whispered something to Judy. Judy frowned and looked back. Kama closed the door behind them, but not before she'd heard Judy say, "But he's dead." She shrugged it off, wondering who they were talking about now.

The museum was quiet and then Kama heard the tapping.

*A flash of green and sky beyond.*

She suddenly realized she'd been hearing it on and off all afternoon, but hadn't really focused on it until now. As her headache had gotten worse, the sound had gotten louder.

*Buzzing and clicking.*

She followed the tapping back to the room housing the Myth and Magic exhibit, but the sounds stopped when she got to the doorway. She waited quietly a moment, thinking it was probably a mouse. When the tapping began again, she peeked inside, trying to locate the direction it was coming from. As soon as her eyes glimpsed the mask in the enhanced lighting, fear clenched her stomach. It was just as she'd remembered it the first time she'd seen it in the underground cave in the jungle. The museum mutated and melted into...

*...jungle, with its heat, humidity, and the sounds of bugs buzzing, clicking, and tapping. She saw his face then. It registered as evil, but she couldn't immediately remember why. A woman sat on a mat next to her, mixing something in a gourd. Kama hugged her aching stomach while the woman made her drink from the gourd. She lost consciousness.*

When she opened her eyes again, she was in St. Agnes Hospital and Linda was rubbing her head. "I was concerned. You haven't been yourself lately—not since you got back. But that remark about Sean worried me. I knew you couldn't have meant that his death was worth so little. I decided to go back to the museum and check on you. I found you on the floor out of your head. You were groaning and holding your stomach. I couldn't get through to you so I called the ambulance. How do you feel now?"

Kama looked up at her and tried to speak but nothing came out. She couldn't reach out and hold Linda's hand or even hang onto consciousness—it began slipping. She closed her eyes and thought back to the museum. *She heard the tapping again*...and remembered walking over to the mask. The tapping was coming from the gourd that had small holes in the top. She lifted the lid and saw a small green snake.

It began coming back in a sickening rush—the trip to the Amazon, finding the tribe, their cave and the secret room with all the unbelievable treasures. She wanted everything but knew the people would never part with the items, but she had determined to at least have the mask—the fabulous mask of a god unlike anything she'd ever seen before.

She should have heeded the warning of the women in the village not to barter for that mask. The sorcerer had said it was taboo for that mask to leave their world, that the gods would be angered. She hadn't listened and found one of the leaders who could be bribed. She'd bartered for the mask and then sent it on to the States before anyone could figure out what she'd done.

She hadn't taken the jungle myths seriously—all illusion, she'd thought. They were convenient stories, a way for the primitives to make sense of their world. Since she didn't believe in their curses they couldn't harm her, right? Except, Sean had broken the taboo of taking pictures of the cave. Shortly after that, he'd died mysteriously in his sleep. She'd convinced herself that it was a heart attack.

And then she'd done the forbidden; she'd taken the mask. But she was all right, she'd made it back—except for the headaches and the stomachache that had begun almost imperceptibly and had gradually gotten worse as the days passed. She remembered the sorcerer giving her the beautiful gourd—a parting gift, she'd thought, some sort of peace offering before she left. When she'd gone back to her tent and opened it, the small green snake inside shot out, biting her before she could react.

*Drums, tapping...*

She'd forgotten about that until today.

*Only today was the illusion. She'd never made it back. She wasn't in a hospital in the States with Linda. She opened her eyes and looked up through the green jungle canopy, to the sky. The pains were worse now. It was too late for the medicine the healer-woman had given her to drink. She felt panicked and helpless, but couldn't move anymore.*

*She saw the sorcerer walking away with the mask, tapping it as if to appease some god that all was well. The mask had never made it back to the States after all, and her efforts had been for nothing, dissolving back into the obscurity of this illusive jungle. She knew now, too late, it hadn't been worth it.*

~

# The Case of the Clay Pigeon

SUNNY FRAZIER

It began like any other July day in Fresno—hot. Holmes was lounging on the settee, smoking a scintillatingly sweet concoction in his meerschaum pipe. I lowered the air conditioner's thermostat slightly, hoping he wouldn't notice until the electrical bill arrived.

There was a timid knock on the door. The housekeeper bustled to open it. A moment later a diminutive young woman stood at the threshold of the study, shivering despite the heat.

"A Miss Holly Funch to see you," the housekeeper announced.

Miss Holly Funch took a seat at the edge of a brocade Queen Anne chair. Holmes studied her intently, which is what he felt was the purpose of a study.

Miss Funch opened her mouth to say something, but Holmes held up a long index finger.

"You are eighteen and a half years old, you are getting married in three weeks to Charles Huntington of the Huntington Drive Huntingtons, and you are worried about a missing statuette." He stopped, put two fingers on his forehead. "A pigeon made of clay, I believe."

"Why, that's astounding!" Miss Funch exclaimed.

I might have thought so, too, if I hadn't observed the *Fresno Bee* lying open to both the social announcements page and the police blotter.

Holmes rang the housekeeper and asked her to bring iced tea.

"Now, how can I help you, Miss Funch?" asked Holmes.

"I need to get the clay pigeon back. It was a gift from my mother-in-law-to-be. She's out of town and hasn't heard that it's missing."

"Is it valuable?"

Here, she hesitated as the housekeeper came in with the tea. "Well, it's a Margaret Hudson. My mother-in-law believes anybody important in this town displays a Margaret Hudson figurine in the foyer or on the dining room table. Why, I've even come across them in the powder room." She blushed slightly. "The problem is, if Mrs. Huntington doesn't see her gift on my table, she will consider it a breach of good manners and is likely to encourage her son to call off the wedding."

"Do you have a photograph of the missing pigeon?"

She handed over a Polaroid of a dune-colored clay bird resting on a doily, as well as a substantial down payment for services not yet rendered.

"We shall begin hunting for your pigeon immediately," Holmes assured her. "It will be gracing your table before the nuptials take place."

After the young lady left, Holmes tossed the photo on the marble-top coffee table. "Take a look at that, Watson. Ugly little duckling, isn't it? Looks as if a five-year-old was turned loose in the Pottery Barn."

I scrutinized the Polaroid. The poor bird did look artistically challenged. "I hear these figurines are prized throughout the city and considered quite the collectible at the moment. But tell me, Holmes, how can you be so sure you'll be able to find the statue in time to save her marriage?"

"I will use a small portion of my stipend to purchase an identical one at the Hudson workshop."

It was a brilliant plan, simple and to the point. As we were chortling over it, we started at the sound of tea glasses slammed onto the tea tray. The housekeeper stomped out of the room.

"What in the world ruffled her feathers?" I wondered aloud.

"Never mind, Watson. We must be off. The game's afoot."

The studio was tucked away in Old Fig Garden in an old adobe abode. In the covered patio, several apprentices sat at tables playing with gray clay. Holmes went up to one such worker and communicated quietly with her while I peered over the shoulder of several artisans, their hands working nimbly and their nails getting grimy.

"Let's be off, Watson," Holmes ordered.

When we were out of the patio area I asked Holmes why he had not bought the clay pigeon, or even checked out the gift shop.

"Clay pigeons haven't been part of the Hudson repertoire since 1997. Nobody in the shop was trained to sculpt the clay pigeon, so they can't reproduce one. And it's highly unlikely anyone would be willing to part with the item. They've become quite valuable."

"Perhaps Margaret Hudson could reproduce the piece?" I suggested.

"Perhaps—but the woman flew the coop three years ago. The staff continues to receive regular instructions conveyed by post."

I could see this piqued Holmes' interest even more than the missing pigeon because it was, after all, the larger mystery. I reminded him that he wasn't being paid to find the creator, just the creation.

Unable to buy his way out of solving the mystery, Holmes headed over to the police department to read the missing pigeon report. The report offered few clues except for the mention of a matronly woman seen in the vicinity of the residence that Ms. Funch and Mr. Huntington would soon occupy.

"Could you run a cross reference check on missing sculptures, specifically missing Margaret Hudson figurines?" Holmes asked the clerk behind the desk. The young woman's fingers flew across the keyboard. The printout revealed thirteen stolen clay pieces: three bears, two otters, five squirrels, two rabbits, and Miss Funch's pigeon. All of the victims were names recognizable on the society page.

"We seem to have a thief intent on cornering the market of clay-rendered animal figurines in the Fresno area," pondered Holmes.

"And perhaps cornering the artist herself," I added, still concerned about the missing Margaret.

Holmes looked at me with a start of recognition. "By Jove, I think you've made a connection, Watson!" With that he was off at a brisk pace and I did my best to keep up.

Our next destination was the home of the artist. Holmes, with his impenetrable powers of deduction, had coerced the artist's address while talking to the young woman at the pottery studio. We drove in his Hillman across town to Kearney Boulevard. The address written on Holmes' shirt cuff matched the one displayed on a rusty mailbox.

"The residence appears deserted," noted Holmes. The fact that we might be trespassing either did not occur to the detective or he ignored the possibility. He jimmied a window at the rear of the house and made entry.

My days of climbing through windows were long past, so I followed through the back door after Holmes opened it. The interior of the house was dusty, as if it had not been occupied in some years. Holmes was taking methodical inventory of each room and its contents. I wandered into the parlor. There were photographs in silver frames on the top of a player piano. Not wishing to disturb anything in the room, I leaned over the piano bench to peer at a portrait of a young girl.

"Watson!"

Startled, I lost my balance and struck a nail protruding from the wood of the piano. Blood ran down my face.

"Dammit, Holmes, look what you've done!"

"You're a doctor, patch yourself up. I wanted to stop you from touching those photographs."

I took a handkerchief out of my breast pocket and dabbed at the wound. "Something appeared familiar about the center photograph. I was just trying to get a closer look," I grumbled.

Holmes took the photo and studied it under his magnifying glass.

"I think you've hit the head on the nail, Watson. There is something familiar in the face of this little girl," Holmes said quietly. He ordered me back to the automobile. I asked if we were going to St. Agnes so I could get a tetanus shot.

"We have more important things to concern ourselves with," Holmes replied.

I'm not a detective in the same league with Holmes, but it took me little time to realize we were headed back to 221B Baker Street. Holmes hurried into his apartment and rang for the housekeeper. I hoped he was ordering up iced tea and scones. It had been a bit of a stressful morning.

When the housekeeper appeared, Holmes wasted no time.

"Madame, do you have something to tell me?" asked Holmes.

"Your friend, Mr. Watson, is bleeding like a stuck pig all over my freshly mopped floor."

"Aside from that. How long have you been working here?" Holmes demanded.

"Why—do you fancy giving me a raise?"

Holmes tolerated her impudence. "I believe it's been three years—around the date of the newspapers left at your house. Tell me, Margaret, why did you give up a life of fame and fortune to become a housekeeper?"

She looked like a startled starling and tried to flee but Holmes caught her by the wrist.

"You've stolen your own sculptures to increase their value. Isn't that true?" accused Holmes.

"Pshaw! I took back what was mine to begin with. My pieces had become collectibles for the wealthy and prominent people, so I took a position of a working class maid to remind myself that art is for the masses."

Mrs. Hudson led us to the gardening shed where she had hidden the clay figurines in bags of potting soil. Holmes called the constable and had Margaret Hudson arrested for thievery and impersonating a housekeeper.

"How in the world did you know it was our Mrs. Hudson all along?" I asked the detective.

"Elementary school, my dear Watson." He explained that the photograph of the child on the piano was taken in a classroom where the name "St. Helen's School" appeared on the blackboard in the background. On her résumé, Mrs. Hudson had listed St. Helen's in her school credentials.

"And if you had looked closely, instead of fussing about your head wound, you would have noticed the modeling clay at the child's desk," Holmes added. "It was an early clue to Mrs. Hudson's future profession."

There's no arguing with genius. I bowed to his superior powers of deduction as he sprawled on the settee and tuned his violin. We'd served justice yet another day, but now had no housekeeper to serve us lemonade. Thirsty and exhausted from the day's adventures, I went to fetch beverages. Being part of Sherlock's life was certainly worth a few sacrifices because, as everyone knows, there's no place like Holmes'.

~

# ~HOLIDAYS CAN BE MURDER~

# Top o' the Mournin'

JO ANNE LUCAS

*An Irish wake is held to fool the devil about a soul's passing.*
*The devil is not a good sport.*

Grampa O'Leary would have loved it—his wake, with the women dressed in their loveliest, the men at their heartiest, the murder, the jewel theft, music, food, dancing—all grand entertainment for his passing.

I'd decked myself out in a green gown by Versace, French perfume, and the famous Spanish Eyes diamond and emerald waterfall necklace I'd inherited from Gramma O'Leary. Just an all-American girl paying tribute to her Irish heritage.

Amid music and loud-pitched conversations at the San Joaquin Country Club I'd been butterflying around from group to group, condoling with friends and chatting up acquaintances, when my hunk-ahoy detector signaled primo specimen within cruising range. Immediately, my eyes locked onto the treacherously handsome Cabe Serrano as he entered the ballroom. He escorted his sister Aurora in, left her with their wraps at the cloakroom, then made his way to me and introduced himself. I thought my brother must have invited him and I made a mental note to thank him later. I shifted back into hostess mode long enough to eyeball the sister Aurora situation. She wore a blue silk designer suit with some serious diamond earrings, I figured them at least 2 carets each. I saluted her taste, but not her sulky face at being left alone. No *problemo*; self-styled letch Stevie Meyers had appointed himself devoted swain. I knew Aurora would be kept busy, so I partnered with Cabe for the heavy breathing sweepstakes.

Between dinner courses Cabe and I made with some sultry slow dancing. Before waiters could completely clear away the pot roast and potatoes, the lights went out. People milled about, bumping into us in the dark. There was an odd brushing at my neck. I grabbed for my necklace too late. I yelled and lunged to catch the culprit, but Cabe held me in his strong arms while he murmured soothing nothings. Cozy, but not addressing the situation. I was considering punching him in the stomach to get away, when there came a loud crashing of chairs and a woman's scream.

Mercifully, the lights came back on. However, the screaming continued. I zeroed in on the source: Aurora Serrano was making with the mouth as she kneeled over Stevie Meyers lying on the floor by their table.

I made my way to her, pushed gawkers aside, and ascertained Stevie was dead. Someone had plunged a steak knife into his chest and left it. Although there was little blood, Aurora'd managed to get splotchy with it.

A waiter brought her some brandy and she left off the screaming and tearfully told her story. Boiled down, it came to this: Someone tried to heist her diamond earrings. Stevie defended her and got offed for his effort. The assailant had gotten away with one earring, upping his take for the evening.

Pretty busy thief.

A shout of discovery turned our attention to the wall by the exit. My necklace and Aurora's earring lay in a heap on the floor.

Hmmm, not only busy, but clumsy, too.

The helpful citizen picked up the jewels and eliminated any useful prints. I took the necklace and put it down on a cleared table. The clasp had been wrenched off and a thread was caught on the stump.

My brother, the not-your-typical-Irish-cop, made like a

good detective and hustled some of his buddies to the scene. Our helpful citizen expounded his theory that the thief had hit the wall in his haste, dropped the loot, and escaped through the exit. Other citizens nodded in agreement. Aurora began bawling again, and Cabe said he was taking her home.

I raised my eyebrows at brother Mike.

"If you don't mind, Serrano, I'd like to hear from Kathleen first," he said.

Cabe ignored him and started for the door with his weeping sister.

"Don't let them go, Mike," I said.

I needn't have worried. Mike signaled a cop to stop their progress and return them to our fold. Cabe protested vehemently and Aurora turned up the waterworks.

I gestured to my crooked Casanova. "Cabe here lifted my necklace, it's probably in his jacket pocket."

That set the cat among the pigeons. Lover-boy tried to break away from the cop's hold. Mike barked out orders for additional restraint and Cabe quieted down.

I moved over and stood in front of Aurora. "And I'm betting you'll find the broken clasp to that other necklace and the missing earring in Cutie-Pie's purse."

Can I call them, or what?

Cabe'd stolen my jewels, and across the room Aurora was to have tossed a fake necklace and one earring against the wall. The idea being to create a disturbance and give Cabe an alibi since I could swear he hadn't left my side. Only, Stevie Meyers being a true-blue letch had hung onto Aurora when the lights went out, so she stabbed him.

As they took the brother/sister act away, I looked down at the fake necklace on the table. Pretty clever plan, I thought. It would have worked except for one thing…you can't fool Tom O'Leary's granddaughter with sham rocks.

~

# True Confections

SUNNY FRAZIER

Except for that one incident with the Godiva chocolates, my marriage would have been perfect.

I had a house on the bluffs in Fresno and my golf game was respectable. My wife wasn't beautiful, but she was intelligent and rich, qualities a man looks for when he climbs the corporate ladder. My marriage had survived the seven-year-itch twice before I hired Marvella to be my secretary. She had an hourglass figure that would make any man rethink his marriage vows. She swiveled in her office chair with hips designed to drive men wild. She lounged seductively on the patio during her endless smoke breaks. Before long, I was drawn into my first affair.

Marvella wasn't demanding. She simply adored me so much that she thought I'd look better behind the wheel of a Corvette than a Lexus. She hinted that she wanted a diamond tennis bracelet, although she never held a racquet in her hand. My cash reserves were soon running low.

Marvella pointed out that murdering my wife was the logical solution to my marital and monetary problems. Between my wife's inheritance and the sizable insurance policy, I'd have plenty of money to spend. Marvella told me to find a foolproof method, but she didn't want to know the details in case the cops came calling.

Committing adultery is one thing—committing murder is

quite another. I knew my wife's habits but now I studied the details of her daily routine. I asked questions, went out with her more often, even went shopping with her to see what products she purchased. She seemed flattered by my attentiveness. Strangely enough, I found myself rediscovering all the wonderful reasons why I married her in the first place.

One of her passions was candy. She stashed half-eaten boxes of chocolates strategically around the house. There were caramels on her nightstand, butter creams next to her reading chair, nougats within reach of the TV, and a slightly soggy box of chocolate-covered cherries in the bathroom.

Valentine's Day was around the corner. Deadly bon-bons would do the job.

Finding just the right poison was difficult. Arsenic had been done to death. Rat poison seemed too trite. What I needed was a lethal liquid, something I could inject through the thin film of chocolate and into the rich center without disturbing the outer appearance of a piece of candy. I located a web site on the Internet where "Jolly Roger" supplied a recipe for making liquid nicotine. When my wife left for a three-day stay at a health spa, I worked in the kitchen shredding cheap cigarettes, soaking the tobacco, and boiling the mass down to a potent amber liquid.

On February 14, I placed the tainted box of Godiva chocolates and a long-stemmed red rose on the dining room table and left for work. I had appointments away from the office all morning just to make sure that Marvella and I weren't seen together. We'd been keeping our distance for two weeks so she'd be in the dark when the murder occurred.

By one o'clock I had to know. I phoned home. My wife picked up on the second ring.

"Did you find the box of candy, sweetheart?" I sputtered. "I know you love Godiva chocolates."

"You've been so romantic these days," she purred, "that I've been dieting. I dropped by the office and gave the candy to your secretary. She seemed delighted when I said they were from you. Lucky girl will never have to worry about her figure. She'd already eaten a dozen pieces before I left."

It was supposed to be the perfect murder—and in some respects, it was.

~

# Grandma's Monopoly

CORA J. RAMOS

I'd still be working for someone else, except for that one incident. It started the morning I was running late because Grandma was winning our daily game of Monopoly she insisted upon with breakfast. When I finally broke away, I ran out the door and into Jeb, our tenant who had recently rented the house in the rear.

"Don't worry about the trash can this morning." Jeb smiled. "I can see you're in a rush. I'll get it and put it out at the curb. And I'll get it back after they pick up."

"Would you? I'd be so grateful—thanks."

There had been a rash of burglaries in the neighborhood lately and I didn't want the house looking unoccupied, especially with Grandma inside. She was so delicate. I wanted no upsets for her.

Before Christmas, Colin Whitfield, Grandma's childhood sweetheart, had begun coming to tea every Wednesday afternoon. He had come back to town after being gone for almost fifty years, a widower and her suitor again. They'd picked up where they must have left off as young people in love.

"Open it now." I heard Colin say this last Wednesday while I was doing dishes in the kitchen.

I peeked around the corner into the dining room and saw a tear in Grandma's eye. She was holding a premiere edition of Monopoly.

"The third one you've given me." She kissed him on the cheek, got up, and went to the shelves that held her collection of board games, the ones she made me play with her daily. She patted them and said, "Samantha's inheritance." She set the new game on the others she'd kept since she was a young girl.

*How sweet. She thinks I love them as much as she. Well, they certainly will always be treasures to me.*

Next morning, running late again, I kissed Grandma on the cheek. "Bye."

"Sit down," Grandma said in a serious tone.

"I can't be late today, Grams, it's Christmas Eve and I've got an important meeting with someone who is going to look at my designs. It might actually mean financing to start production."

"Sit."

I bit my lip and sat on the divan while she went to the game shelf. I looked out the window and watched Jeb sweeping the sidewalk out front. Grandma sat in her Queen Anne chair and lifted the lid off one of the older Monopoly boxes, revealing old costume jewelry among the game pieces. She picked up a green-stoned bracelet and held it up to the light while she talked.

"You could open your own business, now," she said, a twinkle in her eye.

"Sure." I nodded, humoring her. "If I got Boardwalk and Park Place, maybe."

Her memory was failing if she thought those baubles were valuable. It bothered me but I didn't let it show. I knew she was having memory problems, but this made me very uncomfortable about her mental state.

"I really can't play this morning," I said as I hurried out, not wanting to let Grandma see my concern. I ran into Jeb, who was now sweeping the driveway.

"You're so thoughtful. I really appreciate your concern for Grandma's property. Thanks for watching out for her."

"It's what I do." He tipped his cap, smiled and kept sweeping.

That afternoon when I came home, there was a cop car in front and Grandma was in a tizzy. What I had feared had finally happened—the thief had struck. Thankfully Grandma was all right, but rambling on about some missing games.

"Well, now, I have all the information I need, and when we find the robber we will return your games." The detective winked at me.

I sank into the chair ready to cry after he left. Grandma was really losing it. How embarrassing.

Christmas Day, I took Colin aside. "Grandmother's very upset. Please talk to her. She hid her costume jewelry in that old Monopoly game and it's been stolen. There was only costume jewelry in the box—not at all valuable. But she doesn't see it that way."

He became so upset I thought maybe he'd given her an expensive piece of jewelry that she'd hidden among the cheap ones. It was so like her.

Next day, garbage day, I took the Christmas wrap to the trashcan and saw the corner of the old Monopoly game sticking out. I immediately called the police.

Detective Willis, from the Fresno Police Department, returned reluctantly, after I insisted.

"Can you identify this, ma'am?" He picked up the Monopoly box I'd retrieved with a gloved hand.

"Of course it's mine!" Grandma got up and picked it up to put it on the shelf with the others.

"We'll need that for fingerprint evidence. I'm sorry but there was no jewelry found in the trashcan and it seems your renter is nowhere to be found."

"Who cares? At least I have my game back."

I looked at Detective Willis. He shrugged in return.

"Samantha, I've been a silly old woman holding on to memories. I want you to take it now, and all the others, to start your own business." She patted the pile of games.

"They need it for fingerprints, Grams. Proof against Jeb. He must have seen you hold up the jewelry the other morning in the parlor. When you napped, he stole it. Sorry, the jewelry wasn't worth anything—it was costume jewelry."

"You ninny. I don't care about Jeb and the jewelry. That Monopoly set is one of my many originals." She lovingly patted the stack of games again. "Ten thousand dollars here, maybe more. Enough to get you started in that business you wanted. You take them to a dealer and sell them all."

I looked at the wall of games in amazement. There was nothing wrong with her mind.

She laughed. "Why don't we have one last match before you take them. The detective can join us."

Detective Willis smiled as he picked up one of the Community Chest cards. "Seems Jeb missed the most valuable item in the Monopoly set. When we find him he's going to wish he had taken the 'Get Out of Jail Free' card."

~

# Fiesta de los Muertos

SUNNY FRAZIER

The victim, sixteen-year-old Guadalupe Herrera, was found on May 10. She was strangled and her body was dumped in an alley in Parlier. The picture her family gave the deputies showed her with long, black hair. When her body was found, her hair was hacked off close to the scalp.

That had been the first one. Homicide Detective Harvey Wilkerson looked at the spread of files on the desk in front of him. Four murders in the year since the first, all with the same MO: teenage Mexican girls, different towns, waist-length hair missing. "I'm telling you, Lieutenant, we've got the makings of a multiple murderer in the county."

"Fine, Harv," Lieutenant Jacobs snorted. "I'll just march right upstairs to Sheriff Overholt and fill him in on the news."

"I could be right," Wilkerson stubbornly insisted as he thumbed through a folder.

"And you could be wrong," Jacobs countered as he reached in his lower desk drawer and took out a bottle of Jim Beam and two shot glasses. "It could be one man but more likely it's five different men. It's against the laws of nature for one man to kill over and over."

"You never heard of Jack the Ripper?"

"That was a long time ago. This is 1950." The lieutenant tipped the glass back and downed a jigger. "Things like that happen over in those foreign countries—not here in California."

Wilkerson sipped the whisky. "What about Joseph Mumfree, the ax murderer back in the 1920s? And Earle Nelson, the bible-thumper who strangled twenty-two women in '26? Those men killed a slew of women in California."

"Son, those killings occurred in Los Angeles County, and everybody knows people are strange down there. I'm telling you, we don't have a maniac in Fresno County doing this." Lieutenant Jacobs took out a pack of Lucky Strikes and flipped open his lighter. "These Mexican girls were probably done in by their boyfriends. Happens all the time."

"Every one of those young girls was strangled and her hair cut off."

"Probably cultural. We don't know the ways of the Mexicans."

Wilkerson wasn't satisfied with the answer. His gut told him that the hair was tied into the killings somehow. "I'd like a chance to try to find the killer, sir. I've submitted a request for five deputies and a room to work in."

Lieutenant Jacobs snubbed out the cigarette. "Tell you what. I'll give you two deputies. You can use the storage room at the far end of the hall. You've got two weeks to solve the cases. But I don't want any talk of multiple murders leaking out to the sheriff or to the press. No sense in panicking the whole county for nothing."

Wilkerson and his crew of two, Deputy Saunders and Deputy McMaury, cleaned out the storage room. They set up card tables and smuggled a typewriter out of Records Division. Rolling up their sleeves, they got to work.

Wilkerson discovered that few people had been interviewed at the time of the killings. They were migrant workers, for the most part, and it was noted in the reports that they spoke little English. No attempt was made to bring in an interpreter, and none of the investigators in the initial contact spoke a word of Spanish.

"The leads are ice-cold," snapped Deputy Saunders. He and McMaury had spent the afternoon going from farm town to farm town following up clues that didn't exist. "I didn't get much cooperation from the people in the barrio. Most of them don't speak English."

"And the ones that do take one look at the uniform and clam up," added McMaury.

"I know the interviews are a long shot," Wilkerson told the reluctant deputies, "but we have to start somewhere."

In his own mind, Wilkerson questioned why the sheriff was still so resistant to deputizing Mexicans. With the ever-growing Mexican population in the county, the department sorely needed men who could speak Spanish. The city police had already recruited a handful of Mexicans and put them in blue uniforms. But Wilkerson kept his views to himself. He knew the idea was unpopular at headquarters.

The two-week deadline weighed heavily on the trio. They were authorized to put in twelve-hour shifts, which didn't make any of their wives happy.

"Honey, the money will come in handy," Wilkerson sweet-talked his wife, Debbie, when she complained about keeping his supper hot.

"Will you buy me that television set you promised me six months ago?" she asked.

Television was a fad, but that was another opinion Wilkerson kept to himself. Debbie had her heart set on owning one of the ugly boxes. She said it would keep her company as she stayed at home and raised the baby and during the long nights when he worked late. He had his eye on the latest model Mercury coming off the line now that postwar production was making cars affordable. In the meantime, they'd both make do with the radio and the bus lines.

As the first week passed, bits and pieces of information began to pile up. It seemed logical to Wilkerson to lay it out in some manner so all of the information could be read at a glance. One morning Deputies Saunders and McMaury walked into the storeroom and found the wall papered with a photo of each girl as she looked before the murder. Beneath the black-and-white images was the name of the victim, the date of her murder, and the city where the homicide took place. If there was any family information, it was neatly typed and posted on index cards.

Despite the detailed work and his attempt to track the murderer's motives, Wilkerson was nearly out of time. The arbitrary two-week deadline winnowed down to the last twenty-four hours. The other two deputies had long since lost interest in what they considered a hopeless cause. Instead of investigating, they sat at the table and twirled pencils between their fingers, drank coffee, and smoked pack after pack of cigarettes.

On Friday at three-thirty in the afternoon, there was a knock on the storeroom door. Saunders got up to answer it.

"The cleaning lady wants to run a mop over the floor," he announced.

Up to now, Wilkerson's policy had been no unauthorized personnel in the room. As a result, the small area was dusty and needed a good going-over. "Let her come in," he sighed. She might as well get a head start. They wouldn't be needing the storeroom anymore.

Mrs. Castillo muttered under her breath in Spanish as she looked at the overflowing ashtrays and coffee stains on the tables. She bustled around with polish and a rag. The men pretended to be busy and she pretended to be uninterested. But the sight of the information posted on the wall made her stop her cleaning. She looked around the room. Finally, she spoke up.

"Why you have the fiesta days on the wall?" she asked, puzzled.

"Excuse me?" Wilkerson lifted his head from the paperwork in front of him.

"Fiestas." Mrs. Castillo walked up to the first one and tapped a finger on the date of Guadalupe Herrera's death. "*Día de la Madre.*"

Madre. Mother's Day. How had he failed to make the connection? He'd forgotten to buy Mother's Day cards and caught hell for it at home. The date should have stuck in his head. Getting to his feet, he walked toward the next picture, that of Rosa Torres. He put his finger on the date. September 16.

"*Día de la Independencia.* Like Fourth of July, only for Mexico," the cleaning lady informed him.

Around the room they went. There was no way to check the woman's information, but she seemed sure of herself. Little Lucia Orosco had died ironically enough on *Día de los Muertos*— November 2, the Day of the Dead. Consuela Chavez's body was discovered on the sixth day of January, *Día de los Reyes Magos,* Three Kings' Day. The last young woman, Carmen Padilla, was murdered on February 5, which Mrs. Castillo informed him was *Día de la Constitución.* Mexican Constitution Day.

"That's the connection," Wilkerson said to the deputies. "All of the girls were murdered on a holiday."

"Hell, every day's a fiesta to the Mexicans," McMaury shot back.

"It's still a lead." Wilkerson stared at each photograph as he circled the room. "We've got a killer who follows the Mexican holidays, so he's probably Mexican. Mrs. Castillo, when is the next holiday for your people?"

"*Cinco de Mayo.*"

"And what day is that?"

"May fifth. Tomorrow."

Wilkerson felt a chill go through his body. The deputies sat up and let the pencils drop from their fingers.

"He's going to find another victim tomorrow. We've got to stop him," Wilkerson said.

"How can we do that, Harvey?" Saunders got up and walked around the room, jabbing his finger at every listed location. "He never kills in the same city. Parlier, Orange Cove, Del Rey, Malaga, Kerman. We can't be in every city at once."

"I'll talk to the sheriff. Maybe we can get some extra units."

"Harv, this case is unsolvable." McMaury also stood up and clapped his hands on the detective's shoulders. "Give it a rest."

But Mrs. Castillo was tugging at Wilkerson's sleeve. "Señor. The *bolantine de caballitos* comes to town."

"I don't understand." Wilkerson saw the fright in her face. "What are you saying?"

"*Bolantine.*" She pointed to the floor and made a circle with her finger. He still didn't understand. She formed hands into fists and held them in front of her. Bobbing up and down she said, "*Caballitos.*"

"Looks like she's riding a horse," McMaury commented.

"*Sí! Caballitos.*" Again, she made the downward circle in the air.

"Little horses?" Wilkerson said quietly. "Like a merry-go-round?"

Mrs. Castillo nodded with relief and pointed to each name of a town.

"I think she's trying to tell us the carousel goes to a different town every fiesta." Wilkerson turned to his deputies.

"So?" Saunders shrugged. "Why should we care where the merry-go-round shows up?"

"Because maybe the wetback who runs the ride has a thing for little girls," McMaury shot back.

"No Mexican—*gringo.*"

All heads turned to look at Mrs. Castillo. Her eyes flashed in anger. She stroked her face. "*Gringo,*" she repeated.

The carnie was white. He went from town to town with his prancing horses and death followed.

"Tomorrow is another fiesta. Mrs. Castillo, do you know where the..." Wilkerson struggled with the words, "the *bolantine de caballitos* will be?"

"*Sí*, señor deputy. He is in my town. Mendota." Her eyes teared up. "My daughter will go. She has long hair."

On May 5, at first light, Detective Wilkerson, Deputies Saunders and McMaury, along with six patrol deputies, took up positions around the field where the food booths were being set up and a stage for the mariachis was being hastily built. They waited until Daniel Knowles had parked his semi and started to unload the carousel ponies.

"We'd like a word with you," Wilkerson called out as he walked up to the man.

Knowles smirked at the deputies. "What's the matter, officers? Am I parked illegally?"

"No sir," replied McMaury. "But we'd like to ask you a few questions."

Wilkerson let his men do the interview. He walked around the unloaded crates and looked at the pastel ponies. Every one had a long, black tail. Bending down, the detective ran his fingers through the hair.

Human hair.

He stood up and pulled out his handcuffs.

"We got our man," he quietly announced.

~